A Very Merry Hitman

Katie Reus

Dedication

For all my readers who love the holidays as much as me (with a little spice)!

Prologue

Nessa put her palm on the biometric scanner at her aunt and uncle's house and stomped inside, trying to kick her sneakers off before she ran for the kitchen. "Aunt Elli!"

"Hey, kiddo." Her aunt looked up from the big mess on the center island. Her drone was open, with parts lying on a hand towel.

"Oh my god, what happened to Luna?" Luna was the name of her aunt Elli's drone. She used it to spy on people and had taught Nessa to use it like a pro. Nessa was going to be a fighter pilot one day. Or maybe a spy...or maybe she'd play professional soccer first. She hadn't decided. She was only eleven, so she figured she still had time.

"Nothing." Her aunt didn't look up again as she screwed something in place. She had on big goggles that made her eyes look huge. "Just...fixing a couple of bugs. You hungry? We've got snacks in the fridge. Healthy ones too, so I can tell your mom you ate something good over here."

"I'm fine." She was actually starving but had more important things than food to talk about. "Last year you got me the coolest gift ever." Her aunt Elli had introduced her to musical superstar Rebel Martinez. Her friends hadn't believed her until she'd shown them pictures. Now it was all anyone ever wanted to talk about, even a year later.

"Reigning Christmas present champ." Her aunt smiled to herself.

"My mom says that's not a thing."

Aunt Elli looked up at her. "Your mom is amazing and beautiful and I love her...but it's totally a thing."

"I agree. And I have a favor to ask. I know I'm not supposed to ask for presents, but since you're the champ—"

Her aunt shoved up her big mask thing, blinked once as she shook her head. "You can ask me anything." She batted at some of her blonde hair, tried to get it to stay back out of her face.

Nessa took a big breath. "I want a new dad for Christmas."

Her aunt blinked once. Twice. Then again. "You know I'd do anything for you, sweetheart. Your uncle Theo would too. But..." She cleared her throat and for the first time since Nessa had met her, Aunt Elli looked nervous. Or maybe confused.

"I want *Dante* to be my dad. He loves my mom and he loves me and I'm pretty sure my mom loves him too. I don't understand why they're not married. He's at our house *all* the time and he lives so close anyway. Moving in would be easy." She'd realized this summer that it made so much sense. Now she just had to get her mom and Dante to wake up. Sometimes grown-ups just needed a little nudge to see what was right in front of them.

"Ooohhh..." Aunt Elli nodded slowly, then grinned in a way she did when they spied on people. "I think I have an idea."

"I knew you would. That's why you're my favorite." Nessa had only known her aunt a little over a year but she was the coolest person she'd ever met. Super smart according to her grandparents, made a ton of money, gave a ton of it away, *and* she knew Rebel Martinez. Plus she let Nessa spy on people and never snitched. She wasn't like a normal adult.

"I feel like you're manipulating me, but I don't even care. Okay, we're going to get the two of them together because your mom is the nicest human being I've ever met, and against all odds she's into that...Dante."

"Hey!" Nessa loved Dante. He was the absolute best. He always made her mom smile and laugh in a way no one else ever did. And he came to all her school stuff, took her to soccer practice if her mom couldn't, read to her when she asked... It was like he was born to be a dad. *Her* dad.

Her aunt just grinned. "I'm joking. Mostly. He's my rival for your affection. I want to be your number one aunt of *all* time."

"If he becomes my dad, then you'll have no rivals in the aunt or uncle department." Well, except for Uncle Theo, but she kept that to herself.

Her aunt's smile grew even wider. "You're right. Okay, grab some food because I know you're hungry. I have a call to make and we're going to come up with a plan."

CHAPTER 1

*Living my best life? Nope. Living my most
awkward life.*

Aileen felt foolish and scared and all sorts of emotions as she headed up the walk to
Dante's house. He only lived two doors down and was quite possibly the kindest
man she'd ever known.

If she didn't know that he was a hitman, she'd have never in a million years
guessed his profession.

Just like no one other than the people living in her neighborhood knew that
everyone in the near vicinity were all hitmen. Or married to them. In her case,
she was related to them—her mom, dad and brother. And now Elli knew since
she'd married Aileen's brother Theo, but Elli wasn't a hitman. She was an expert
in explosives though.

And Aileen definitely didn't want to think about them right now. Nope.

Not with what she was about to do.

She didn't even get a chance to knock or ring the bell. Dante swung the door
open, his expression concerned. And, you know, *gorgeous*. Everything about the
big man made everything inside her wake up and take notice. Always had. "Hey,
is everything okay? I saw you on the door camera."

Oh, right. Everyone here also had incredible perimeter security. He'd probably
gotten an alert about her before she'd made it up the sidewalk. "Everything's

good." She glanced over her shoulder, saw a couple neighbors out fiddling with their holiday decorations. "Can we talk inside?" she asked as she turned back to the tall, huge and mouthwateringly handsome man who starred in all her fantasies.

Dante was big all over and she assumed it extended...to other places.

"Of course." He stepped back so she could walk inside. "Can I take your coat?" he asked oh so politely.

She didn't want polite Dante. She wanted him growling, naked and underneath her, but one step at a time, she reminded herself. "No, I can't stay long. But..." Oh god, now that she was here inside his lightly decorated house with the scent of cinnamon wafting on the air, she froze. She wasn't sure how to even say the words. "So...you know what happened to me..." She cleared her throat. "Ah..." She didn't want to spell it out, didn't even want to think about the past. But she needed to make sure he understood the context of her request.

"I know." His expression went dark, his jaw flexing slightly.

She'd been roofied in college, didn't actually remember the assault, but had ended up pregnant as a result. And she would never, ever regret Nessa. But Aileen had been broken for a while, messed up in the head. No more. She was tired of living half a life, and she knew Dante could help her move on to the next step. She wanted to feel whole again, to be comfortable in her own skin again.

"Look...my request is kind of selfish and I'm already regretting this." She covered her face with her hands, took a deep breath and faced him again. It was difficult to look directly at him sometimes because he was so intense, always focused on her when she spoke. Because the man actually listened. To *everything*.

"Take your time. Are you sure you don't want to come in and sit?" His voice was soothing, deep and erotic all on its own. Much like the hard man who'd honed every part of his body to perfection. He had to be sharp and deadly, a weapon in every sense of the word.

Just get it out, she ordered herself. "I want to have sex again or at least try and I'm scared to do it with a stranger. I thought maybe I could hire someone professional but that's scary too and I was hoping maybe you could help me. With *sex*," she added when he just stared down at her, looking like a deer caught in the proverbial headlights. Or maybe a wolf caught in headlights.

Probably because she'd propositioned him for sex at four in the afternoon like a total weirdo. He'd probably thought she was coming over to ask for help with her Christmas decorations.

Oh god, this was the longest anyone had not talked, ever. The silence stretched on for an eternity. Birthdays came and went as he stared down at her with those dark, enigmatic eyes and—*bang, bang, bang*.

She jumped at the sound of thumping on his front door, realized that nope, she wasn't old and gray. That it had just felt like an embarrassing eternity.

"Moooom! We've gotta go. Can't be late for soccer if I'm gonna dominate the World Cup one day."

"You know what—just forget I said anything," Aileen muttered to Dante who was still sorta staring at her, his eyes wide and a little wild. Clearly she'd embarrassed him.

And myself.

This was why she shouldn't be around other humans. "Please forget this," she whispered. She turned, swung the door open to find the light of her life standing on the front porch in all her gear. Except her cleats of course. Those would already be packed in the car, along with her ball and bag. Because Nessa was the most organized person she'd ever met and she was only eleven.

Her red curls were tamed into twin braids, her expression one of exasperation. "We can't be late again."

"We've been late one time. *One* time. *Last* year." And her child had never let her forget it. She stepped onto the front porch. "See you later, Dante."

"Oh, Dante, you want to come to practice?" Nessa asked, not deterred one bit. "Sure—"

"He can't. He's busy." She grabbed Nessa's hand and didn't look back because no way was she spending the next couple hours with him after the most awkward non-response ever. She couldn't even turn around and look at him. Seriously, if there was ever a time for a sinkhole to come along, now was it. Just open up, swallow her whole and end her embarrassment forever. She lived in Florida; it was definitely possible.

"Oh, see ya later, Dante." Nessa waved over her shoulder, then looked up at Aileen. "And you know that if you're not early, you're late."

"I know you and Uncle Theo think that."

"And we're right." Nessa dropped her hand and raced toward their driveway, slid into the passenger seat.

By the time Aileen made it to the driver's side, she thought for sure Dante would be back in his house. But nope, he was still standing on the porch watching her.

And looking far too sexy doing it. He was wearing a T-shirt, because Miami winter wasn't all that cold for a man made of pure muscle, clearly. She slid her sunglasses on even though she didn't really need them. But it was a very nice barrier.

"Is everything okay, Mom?"

Nessa's voice pulled her back to the present and she nodded as she put her little car in drive. "Yep. Perfect."

***

"Hey, Elli." Aileen answered her cell as she walked around the track next to Nessa's practice field. Her daughter practiced soccer a couple times a week at a huge athletic center so Aileen used that time to get her walking in and catch up on audiobooks instead of just sitting and watching Nessa play. For her games though, she was all in and never moved from her seat as she cheered.

"Hey, how's practice?"

"Good. Last I saw, Nessa had scored three times." The group her daughter played with weren't supercompetitive, but that didn't stop Nessa. When she wanted to do something, she had to be the best. Something she definitely got from her grandparents.

"That kid's gonna take over the world one day. And I'm going to scoop her up before someone else does. Maybe I'll just create a job for her."

"She's eleven, Elli."

"I know, I know." Her new sister-in-law laughed lightly. The woman was a certified billionaire, or at least her company was since they'd gone public a couple years ago.

She didn't act like one, and gave away so much of her money it was mind-boggling. Aileen only knew because Theo had told her. And she also didn't care that she'd married into a family of hitmen. Elliana fit in better than Aileen did, if she was being honest.

"I'm calling because I have a sort of weird question," Elliana said. "And I never want to overstep but I have this friend who is single and adorable and...I wanted to know if you were maybe interested in meeting up with him. No pressure though. Your mom said you weren't really into dating, but then my friend saw your picture and asked if you were single so... Stop me if I'm out of line."

"Oh, no. I'm just thinking. It's been a while since I've been on a date." Years and years. She'd tried dating when Nessa had been about four, but it had been one disaster after another. And at the end of the day she'd realized that she couldn't bring someone normal into her family anyway. It would never work. So she'd stopped trying. "I don't know." But the timing seemed good, especially considering her awkward proposal to Dante, and super fun rejection. Maybe this was a sign that she needed to say yes.

"Okay, I get that. But he was in explosives like me before and his job is...unconventional. He has no idea about Theo or anyone else, but I'm just saying that if things go well, maybe one day, I don't know, you could bring him into the fold like Theo did with me."

Aileen was pretty sure that Elliana was a unicorn, but found herself saying, "Okay."

"For real? Oh my gosh, you're not going to regret this. I'll send you his information. And if you tell Theo this, I'll deny it, but the man is gorgeous."

Aileen laughed lightly. Her brother could definitely be a bit over-the-top where Elli was concerned. "My lips are sealed. So...he's nice?"

"He's the best, like a big, sweet teddy bear."

"I like the sound of that." If anything, she could just get back out there. Nessa was eleven and would eventually move out and start her own life, as she should. Not too soon, thankfully, but Aileen didn't want to be alone forever. She didn't want what one monster had done to shape the rest of her life.

She'd already given him too much power, and the man was dead. She needed to take back *her* power, her sexuality. Even if it was a little terrifying.

"That's great. I'll send you his information and vice versa."

"Sounds good, thank you. Seriously. I'm so glad that Theo met you."

"You don't have to thank me. I just want you to have every wonderful thing you deserve."

She found herself smiling as she walked around the track. Elli had a way of making everyone feel good about themselves. "Well I'm going to thank you anyway— Oh, there's the whistle. The kids are wrapping up, but I might reach out later about this."

"Perfect, I'll talk to you soon."

As she hung up, Aileen pushed down the weird sensation of...was that guilt? Why on earth did she feel guilty? She'd just agreed to go on a date with someone, that was it.

And clearly Dante had been horrified by her request. Which, okay, she'd sprung it on him with no warning. But as she replayed everything from two hours ago, she winced at herself.

Nope, no coming back from that, at least not today. She needed some distance and then she'd apologize and hope things went back to normal...ish. She just wasn't sure how she was ever going to look him in the eyes again.

CHaPTer 2

*If you'll excuse me, today's bad decisions
aren't going to make themselves.*

"Thanks for coming over," Nestor murmured as he rolled out his cleaning kit onto the kitchen island next to his array of weapons.

"Of course." Dante had been working with Nestor for years and rarely said no to the man. It also didn't hurt that he was Aileen's father—and Dante hadn't talked to her since Wednesday.

Two. Long. Days.

He'd called her once and she hadn't answered. He hadn't wanted to overstep so he'd been…looking out his window and at his security cameras with an obsession that probably wasn't healthy just in the hopes that he'd see her. Maybe "casually" run into her—and continue the conversation she'd started. "Where's Lorna?" he asked instead of pouring out everything in his head.

"Christmas shopping with my angel."

Dante smiled as he picked up the nearest SIG, started breaking it down to clean it. They'd done this so many times together it was second nature. "Is Nessa shopping for herself or others?" he asked, knowing the man's "angel" was the one and only Nessa.

Nestor, a hard, quiet man, actually smiled. "Probably a bit of both."

"I bought her a couple things already, but might add to it. She told me that a girl can never have too many cleats."

Nestor snorted. "So, what do you think of the job next month?"

"I'll take it." This month he was off—he didn't work during December. Or very little, since Nessa was off school and Aileen loved Christmas. But the January job paid a lot of money so he wouldn't turn it down.

Before he'd met Aileen, and everyone else he now considered family, he'd never turned down a job. But since meeting her years ago…things had changed for him. He wanted to be present for her, even if they were just friends. Though he wanted a hell of a lot more and worried that he'd screwed up his big chance to take things to a new level.

No.

He refused to just accept that. He could fix his stupidity and make it clear that he was open to anything she wanted. Even if she terrified him on a level he couldn't define. "Anything else I need to be aware of?"

Nestor paused, shook his head. "Jobs are steady. Nothing on our radar we need to worry about."

Dante wasn't sure what to make of the pause, because it had felt almost charged. Nestor and Lorna, both retired-ish hitmen, now ran a lot of the admin stuff for everyone in the neighborhood. And beyond. Not all of their allies—or coworkers, as he thought of them—lived here. But those who did had created a tight community. All their kids went to a private school literally created for them, and as a rule, they were wary of outsiders. Some of the homes even had underground tunnels between them as escape hatches.

Because all of them had escape plans for if the shit ever hit the fan. They had new identities set up, other homes or bolt-holes to retreat to. It would be insanity not to. He himself had four bolt-holes.

A couple hours later, as they were wrapping up, Nestor glanced at his buzzing phone. "Lorna's almost home with Nessa."

Dante picked up his pace, sliding the last pistol into its case for Nestor. The older man plucked it up and the remaining two and headed upstairs to store them behind the secret wall panel in their bedroom. Nessa didn't exactly know what they did. She thought they did top secret stuff and that was that. For now. One day when she was a little older, maybe they'd explain things, but not now.

Dante was washing his hands at the sink when Nessa came stomping in.

She smiled widely when she saw him, ran straight at him and bear-hugged him. "Dante!"

He pretended to stumble back from the impact. "Hey, kiddo. Buy me anything good?" he asked when she stepped back.

"You know it!" She picked up the big brown bag she'd dropped earlier, then slung it up onto the countertop. It landed with a thud. "But you can't have it till Christmas Day. You know the rules."

He chuckled. "I was just joking, but now I'm curious."

"Well you're gonna have to wait. So what's for dinner?"

"Ah...pizza?" He glanced past her to the mudroom, hoping to see Lorna—and Aileen. Dante hadn't mentioned Aileen to Nestor, and he hadn't wanted to be obvious and ask about her. No one knew how he felt about her and he'd never wanted to make things awkward. But her proposition the other day changed everything, and now all he could think about was the two of them naked together.

"No pizza." Lorna shook her head as she strode in. "Go grab the rest of the bags," she murmured to Nessa as she carried in something that smelled amazing.

Dante recognized the logo of one of his favorite Cuban restaurants on the outside. "You got enough in there for me?"

"Of course." She snorted softly as she set the bags on the countertop. "Grab a bottle of red from the pantry. That child has worn me out, and I know you and Nestor must be hungry."

Nestor stepped into the kitchen at that moment, smiling in a way he only did around his wife. He murmured something too low to hear as Dante ducked into the pantry.

A small pang hit him in the chest, twisted hard. He wanted what they had, but not with just anyone. With Aileen. She was everything he'd never even dreamed existed—kind, a fierce mother who would take on the world for her daughter, smart, and yes, beautiful. So beautiful it hurt to look at her sometimes.

After waiting a solid minute, he stepped back into the kitchen, two bottles in hand because he wasn't sure which Lorna would want. He held them up as Nestor unloaded the foodstuff.

"The Beaujolais," she said, pointing to the one on the left.

As he rummaged around for the bottle opener, he said, "Is Aileen coming tonight?" Did that sound casual?

"Nope," Nessa said as she raced back into the kitchen. "I left the bags in the laundry room so no one would peek," she told Lorna.

"Good girl." Lorna kissed the top of her head. "Now go wash your hands."

"My mom has a date," Nessa said as she stood at the sink pumping soap out. "With some hot, rich guy."

Lorna snickered. "Hot, rich guy?"

"I dunno. That's what I heard her say on the phone."

That...didn't sound like Aileen at all. Dante tried to breathe past the ache in his chest. She was dating? She'd just asked him...for something he'd only ever dreamed about. Though not quite in the way she'd approached him. He'd been so stunned he hadn't been sure how to respond. But he was planning to.

And now she was going on a *date*? Dante needed to know more about this loser.

"Your mom didn't say that." Lorna shook her head as she poured water for Nessa.

"Well, she didn't say hot, but she did say handsome. And he also donates to the same charities as her or something. He sounds like a nice guy."

Dante's hand clenched around the bottle opener. No one was watching him, so he slipped it into his pocket. "I'm gonna grab a bottle opener from home. I'll be back." He hurried from the kitchen before they could protest or say they had another one.

But instead of heading home, he headed straight for the house of his nemesis. He found Elliana in her front yard punching a big blow-up Santa in the face.

The tall blonde looked up in surprise when she saw him.

"Why are you punching Santa?" he asked, momentarily distracted.

"He knows what he did."

Ooookay, then. He shook his head. "I need help." Dante wished he was eating glass right now, but this was how far he'd fallen. Asking help from *her*. His archrival.

Elliana frowned at him, blinked once, then looked over her shoulder and back at him. "Do you think I'm someone else?"

He resisted the urge to roll his eyes. Mainly because he wasn't surprised by her response. Under normal circumstances he'd have never come to Elliana for anything—she was trying to steal his spot as Nessa's favorite relative. And was dumb enough to think she'd won just because she knew some famous pop star. And yes, he realized he sounded like a petulant teen. "Aileen is on a date and I would like to spy on her."

Elliana grinned in a way that sent a shock of terror down his spine. *His*—a hitman feared for his accuracy. But there was seriously something wrong with this woman. Which was why she was perfect to ask for help. "What tools do you need? NVGs, C-4—"

"No. None of that." Not yet anyway. He would not kill Aileen's date. He wouldn't. Wouldn't, wouldn't, *wouldn't*. Probably.

"You sure?" Her grin was pure Cheshire cat.

"Yes I'm sure, you lunatic. Are you going to help me or not? I don't even know where they're at." He was going to find out though.

"Well I do. Come on." She motioned for him to follow her inside her and Theo's house.

She grabbed her car keys and sweater from a set of hooks by the door, then headed through the house and into the garage. He had a feeling the only reason she was helping him was because Theo was out of town for a couple days. Probably why she'd been terrorizing one of the blow-up decorations too.

"Also, you owe me now," she said as they slid into her SUV, sounding far too pleased with herself. "At the neighborhood Christmas party this year, you're going to sing karaoke of my choosing. Springsteen's 'Dancing in the Dark' for everyone to see. With feeling! That's my payment."

"You had that one in the chamber," he muttered even as he pulled his cell phone out.

As he texted Nestor to tell him that something had come up and he wouldn't be back for dinner, he simultaneously wondered if he'd just made the biggest mistake of his life. But no, the biggest mistake of his life would be letting Aileen slip through his fingers. He'd do anything for her, even humiliate himself.

CHAPTER 3

Live every day like it's Taco Tuesday.

Aileen smiled at Diego, her blind date who'd made her feel comfortable from the first moment. There wasn't a spark exactly, but she knew that could take time. She was just getting up in her head because of her proposition to Dante.

Well, she was in her head because of his rejection. Could standing there and staring in horror be considered a rejection? If not, him not speaking to her since said rejection certainly was one. Though to be fair she'd sort of been avoiding him.

Ugh. She mentally face-palmed herself. He'd definitely rejected her. Clearly she'd misread some things between them. But instead of dying of embarrassment, she was moving on. Taking back control of her life. And the next time she saw him, she would pretend everything was normal. Even if it wasn't. Oh god, hopefully he wouldn't want to talk about anything.

"This is a really cute place," she said as the server set different cakes in front of them.

Her date had chosen a mini tuxedo cake and she'd chosen a pink velvet with buttercream frosting that she wanted to bury her face in. She'd show restraint, but oh my god, it looked so amazing. So even if the date was crap, she was getting cake. She called that a win.

"I thought something simple might be easier for a first date, and we can walk along the water later if you want. Or you can bail early and no hard feelings—this is a great place to eat my feelings if you decide I'm a terrible date," Diego said with a laugh.

She snort-laughed at his words. She hadn't been sure what to expect, but it wasn't this humorous man who Elliana had assured her was basically a perfect human being. He was also easy on the eyes, so there was that. He was polished, clean cut, and if she had to guess, was a runner. He had that lean, strong build. But...there was just no spark. "So did you pick this place or did Elli?"

"It was all Elli," he said, laughing. "She told me you loved cake and coffee or tea, and that if I made you uncomfortable for even one second, she'd cut the brakes in my car."

Aileen froze, a bite of cake held in midair. "I feel like you're not joking."

"Not joking." He lifted a shoulder casually, speared some of the dark frosting and white cake on his plate. "Elli's always been overprotective of the people in her life. She saved my ass more than once overseas."

The fact that he called her Elli and not Elliana said a lot in Aileen's book. Elli was particular about who she let into her life. For the most part she didn't seem to like people. Or maybe she was wary of them, was a better description. But she knew that Diego had been adjacent to Elli in some sort of official military capacity that she'd refused to give Aileen details on. "That I definitely believe. She's the most fearless person I've ever met."

"True. But I want to talk about you. So tell me more about this ASMR stuff."

She blinked, not realizing Elli had told him about that. Aileen was an ASMRtist and had a pretty big following online. "Oh, well, first I should say that there are different types of ASMR out there." She'd never had anyone really ask her about her job because the people in her life knew about it and it wasn't something that normally came up in conversation. People in her everyday life outside of her circle knew that she made "YouTube videos to help people sleep" and that was the way she liked it.

He nodded, listening intently in the same way Dante did. *Dang it, no. No thoughts of Dante.*

She cleared her throat, wondering if she really was ready for this whole dating thing. Because it meant she had to actually open up, talk about herself, be personable. Even if she wasn't related to or friends with a bunch of hitmen, it was still part of her nature to keep her life private.

"I'm going to give you the basic description of what it is. ASMR is an acronym for autonomous sensory meridian response. It describes that sensation you might get from different visual stimuli. Or auditory stimuli. Have you ever been listening to an audiobook or watching a late-night infomercial and gotten sort of, like, tingly? Like your whole body is relaxed or your head feels tingly in a sort of relaxing way and you just want to sleep?"

He nodded, laughing lightly. "Yeah, when I can't sleep, I watch a certain online shopping network. I have a couple saved. I have no idea why, but something about the host's voice makes me tired. I have no interest in the jewelry they're selling but something about those videos knocks me out every time."

"That's essentially ASMR. There's a lot of unintentional ASMR out there too—there are a couple quilting tutorial videos I personally use to get to sleep. But a lot of the more mainstream 'triggers' are tapping on various surfaces, scratching, crinkling paper, turning the pages of books or magazines or whatever. There's a lot of research that suggests that ASMR releases endorphins or other neurohormones that help us relax."

"And this is what you do for a living? Make videos?" There was no judgment in his voice, only curiosity.

"Yeah, I've gotten to the point where I bring in enough income from sponsors to pay my bills." More than enough, but she wasn't going to tell him that. She was proud that she'd turned her hobby, something she'd once used to help channel her trauma, into an actual job. Not just a job, but something she loved and was able to help others with. It wasn't a typical career, but it worked well for her schedule. And she didn't have to talk to people if she didn't want to.

"That's incredible. If you don't mind me asking more questions, how did you get into it?"

"I sort of fell into it after I had my daughter." Not exactly the truth. She'd been dealing with PPD and trauma from her attack, then her rapist having the audacity to take her to court for partial custody after he'd been found not guilty. That time in her life had been the darkest she could have imagined. She'd had insomnia, had been in this constant state of panic, and she'd stumbled across a forum about ASMR during one of her late-night attempts to find a way to fall asleep. It had changed her entire life and she would always be grateful for that.

She cleared her throat, banishing her darker thoughts, not wanting to think about the past right now. Or ever. That chapter was behind her and she was ready to take the reins of her life again.

"I was struggling with sleep and stumbled across some videos that helped with insomnia. At the time I was home a lot with my newborn and thought I'd try making some videos of my own. I don't even show my entire face. Originally I did it out of privacy and now it's part of my 'brand.' The whole thing was very therapeutic and then I started getting so many followers. Another ASMRtist mentioned my channel as one of her favorites and that's what sort of kicked things off for me. I reached out to thank her and then we ended up collaborating a couple times. We're still friends to this day. And for the record, there's some very odd ASMR out there. I'm not knocking it, but there is definitely a very small subset of weirdos who are into it for kink or whatever." She shrugged. "So there you go."

"That's incredible." He smiled warmly at her, and nope, no butterflies. But whatever—he was nice and handsome and Elli liked him, so that counted for something.

She was at max capacity for talking about herself. Clearing her throat, she said, "Tell me more about you. I know you served with Elliana but I don't know much more than that." And Elli was always so secretive about stuff.

Over the next half hour, they ate cake, had hot tea and got to know each other. And the entire time she wished it was Dante with her instead.

But she knew what wishing got you. Exactly nada. So she buried her feelings down deep and paid attention to the man in front of her.

CHAPTER 4

Have you ever had one of those days where
you're holding a stick and everyone looks
like a piñata?

"So this isn't like a date-date." From his hiding spot with Elliana in the hat and sunglasses shop full of nonsense items, Dante watched as Aileen laughed at something her sort of good-looking date said.

This wasn't an upscale or intimate place, simply a coffee and dessert establishment in a small shopping area. It was surrounded by what was basically an outside mall. Nothing intimate at all about what he was seeing. Nope. The little fairy lights above them *might* be considered romantic. But it looked like she was giving the guy pity laughs. So there was that.

"She's giving him pity laughs," he growled, trying to convince himself more than Elliana.

"I dunno. Looks like a date to me. And those laughs are real." Elliana had on a hat with mouse ears and giant sunglasses as she turned to him. "What do you think? Can I pull this off?"

He lifted his phone and took a picture of her. Then he texted Theo. He didn't understand why Theo had married this lunatic. Then he looked back at Aileen and Lucky Bastard. "Do you think that guy is good-looking? Just academically speaking."

Elliana slid on a hat with a T-Rex on top, the tail swishing back off her head.

"If I didn't know and love Theo...I probably wouldn't kick him out of bed for eating crackers."

Dante looked down and realized he'd crushed the sunglasses in his hand. *Oops.* He turned to find a sales associate staring at him, eyes wide. He handed over the broken pieces. "I'll pay for it and whatever else she gets." He motioned to Elliana.

The woman simply nodded and took the broken sunglasses with a sniff of disapproval. *Yeah well, get in line, lady.* The majority of the world likely disapproved of him. But he'd given up caring what anyone thought of him by the age of twelve.

"You're not allowed to touch anything else breakable," Elliana murmured as she moved to another little spinning stand, grabbed sunglasses that had fake eyeballs popping out, and cackled as she slid them on.

"Why does this place even exist?" he muttered, looking across the way at the dessert bar. From their angle, they had a decent view of Elliana and Lucky Bastard. Or maybe he was simply Mr. Dead Man.

Yeah, Dante liked the sound of that a lot better. How had she even met this guy? She hadn't said anything about meeting someone new, and here she was on a date with some rando.

"Because it's fun."

"Punching that guy in the throat would be fun."

Elliana tugged off her hat and glasses and grabbed his arm. "Okay, people can hear you. Come on. We're getting out of here because if she sees you, you'll blow your game plan."

He frowned at her even as they headed to the register. "Game plan?"

"Yeah, to win Aileen over. To marry her. Make babies with her. Take family vacations."

He was very aware of the salesperson watching them curiously, but he simply dropped a bunch of cash on the countertop. "You're making a lot of assumptions." None of them were wrong though.

"Yeah, based on observation and facts." She tossed in two candy bars and the dinosaur hat. "He's getting these too," she said to the woman.

"Are those for Nessa?" he asked.

"Nope. These are for me." She grinned and ripped open one of the candy bars as he added more money to the countertop.

"I don't have a game plan," he said as they finally exited the store, making sure to stay out of sight of Aileen.

His only plan had been following her date. And now that he thought about it, he realized it was messed up. He didn't actually care that it was, but yeah. He kept his ball cap pulled low, but it didn't matter because Aileen never looked away from her date once.

Yeah, he really wanted to punch that guy. Dark hair, nice enough face, a stupid-looking sweater and slacks. "Do you know who this guy is? How did she meet him? Did anyone vet him?"

"I trust Aileen to be a grown-up and take care of herself."

Elliana tugged him into what turned out to be a place that sold incense and candles. *Ugh.* The scents were overwhelming, but it was a good place to spy. There were so many people milling about, buying last-minute gifts for the holidays, that they blended easily enough into the crowds.

He stood in the window, watching through one of the blue and white Hanukkah displays as the server brought Aileen and the guy a check. At least the guy picked it up immediately so he wasn't totally horrible. Wait, no, that wasn't good. What if she wanted to see him again?

"As soon as they leave, we're getting out of here. Because it's clear you don't have a game plan. And besides, this is just an intel-gathering op." Elliana handed him a blue candle that said it smelled like the ocean. "You're buying that for me."

"Fine." Not even glancing at her, he handed her his wallet.

Okay now the guy was placing his hand at the small of Aileen's back. *Touching* her. Dante didn't realize he was moving until Elliana grabbed his arm and pulled him back.

"Nope. Acting like a caveman and going all postal or whatever on him is not the right move—"

A scream drew his attention back across the street. A Santa was wrestling with Aileen, grabbing her small purse from the table. As Dante sprung into action, the

Santa shoved her into her date, sending them both flying into one of the outdoor mosaic tables.

A red haze descended over Dante as he gave chase, dodging people as he sprinted after the Santa—who was ridiculously fast.

The guy moved like liquid despite the big, awkward costume, dodging a stroller, then he grabbed onto the edge of a railing and hurled himself over it, parkour style.

What. The. Hell.

Dante reached the railing, watched as the guy landed in a roll on the concrete below, then sprinted in the direction of the nearby marina.

He also realized that people were now watching. Paying attention.

Not something he wanted in his line of work.

He turned away from the scene Santa had made and headed back in the direction of the dessert bar to find Elliana talking to Aileen and her stupid-looking date. Who was now covered in tea.

Heh.

"Aileen, are you okay?" He nudged Elliana out of the way, did a visual sweep of the woman he'd been in love with for years even as he barely skated his hands down her shoulders and arms.

"I'm fine. That was...just nuts. Are you okay?" she asked, green eyes wide.

He nodded. Of course he was okay. "Do we need to cancel your cards or your phone—"

She shook her head as she held up her cell, then patted the front pocket of her snug-fitting black pants. "I put my cash and card in here. That clutch just had...makeup and stuff." Her cheeks flushed pink and he wondered at that, but shelved it for the moment.

"I'm not sure if anyone has called the cops," her date said, interrupting them, his cell phone in hand.

Dante tried to keep his expression neutral when he wanted to throw more than hot tea on the guy.

"Cops can't do anything I can't so don't bother calling them," Elliana said all matter-of-fact to Aileen's date.

Date. Date. Date.

The guy blinked, then nodded slowly as he slid his phone away. "Oookay."

Aileen laughed nervously, then turned away from Dante toward the guy who was definitely going to get throat-punched later. "I'm sorry about the way our date ended."

The guy shook his head. "I'm the one who's sorry. That guy came out of nowhere. I'm just glad you're okay." He turned to Dante then, held out his hand. "And thank you for chasing after him. That was a solid thing to do. We're lucky you were here."

Dante blinked, then grudgingly shook the bastard's hand. Probably squeezed a little too hard, not that the dark-haired man seemed to notice. He was all easy smiles for Aileen.

"Listen, I just got a late work emergency. Aileen, can you take Dante home?" Elliana asked.

He should probably protest, say he wasn't going to interrupt her date. But yeah, that wasn't happening.

"Ah...yeah." She nodded, looking between the three of them before Elliana hugged and kissed her cheek before dashing off, bags of random things he'd bought in her hands. Belatedly he wondered if she still had his wallet.

"It's getting late anyway," the man said as he accepted the receipt and his credit card from the server who still looked a little stunned. Someone had picked up the table and fallen silverware and someone else was currently sweeping up the shards of the broken plates.

Most of the diners had gone back to their desserts so Dante figured no one had called the cops. Sounded about right—people didn't want to get involved. And normally he judged that, but right about now he was using it to his advantage. Or maybe someone had called and they needed to get the hell out of here.

"Okay, well thank you for tonight. It was lovely...except for the Santa mugging," Aileen said as she turned back to the guy who was impossibly getting better looking as they stood there.

Dante felt like a giant next to the other man.

"I'll call you tomorrow? We can talk about the gala?" the guy asked.

"Sounds good." She nodded at him, smiling all sweetly even as Dante moved to stand in between them, started guiding her out of the outdoor seating area.

"What are you doing?" she asked through gritted teeth, her tone low.

What the hell had that guy meant by gala? He made a note to ask her about it later. "Just trying to get you out of here in case someone actually called the cops or security."

"Oh, right..." She glanced around, her cheeks slightly flushed. "I can't believe that happened. That Santa popped up out of nowhere like a total maniac."

"Did he say anything or..." Dante kept his hand at the small of her back as they headed in the opposite direction the bad Santa had run. There were a lot of shops still open, especially so close to Christmas, and he figured they could stop in a few.

Anything to spend time with her and erase the memory of her date.

Because that was the last time she was going out with that guy. Or anyone else.

"No. Wait, do you think it was something...to do with the family?" She lowered her voice even though "Jingle Bells" was blasting over speakers and people were now pouring out of a nearby movie theater. As if some lunatic Santa hadn't just mugged Aileen and created havoc a few stores back.

"I kind of doubt it. Probably saw an easy grab. That purse was expensive." He should know, he'd bought it for her a couple birthdays ago. It was from a well-known luxury brand and one he knew she'd had her eye on but would have never bought for herself. She was too practical sometimes and he'd wanted to spoil her.

"Oh...right. Oh my god, of course that's what he was after." She rubbed her hand over her face. "I'm so dumb, I can't believe I didn't think of that."

"You're not dumb," he muttered. "You've just had a shock. We'll find out who took your purse." Her parents were going to be pissed. And he had no doubt that Elliana had already told Nestor and Lorna and they were probably plotting ways to hurt that foolish Santa.

"That sounds a little murdery. Whatever. We're just going to let this go," she murmured, then looked up at him as if she'd just realized something. "Wait, were you out shopping with Elli?"

He lifted a shoulder, not wanting to lie to her. Ever. So he just answered vaguely. "She has really strange taste. She bought a pair of fake sunglasses with eyeballs that pop out."

Aileen laughed, the lyrical sound rolling over him. "I went Christmas shopping with her a couple weeks ago and it was like shopping with a thirteen-year-old. She's so much fun."

He just grunted.

Aileen linked her arm with his. "Come on, you know you love her."

Then she seemed to realize that she was touching him and started to pull away so he placed his hand over hers. "Are we going to talk about the other day?" he asked quietly.

She tugged again so he let her go, but followed as she walked into a nearby shop that sold winter gear. It seemed a waste for somewhere that had relatively mild winters but the place was busy.

Aileen grabbed a pink and white toque and pulled it all the way over her face. "We can talk about it like this." Her voice was muted as she spoke.

Laughing lightly, he tugged the knit cap off her head, resisting the urge to touch her mussed red hair. She'd left it down tonight in soft, big curls—clearly for her date. "We've been friends for a long time." Though he'd always wanted more. A secret he'd kept to himself because he hadn't wanted to ruin things between them or her family. Plus he hadn't thought she was ready to date again. Her proposition had stunned him. In the best way possible.

She turned away and started looking at scarves. "Yeah, and that's why this is so embarrassing. I'm going to plead temporary insanity."

He glanced over his shoulder when he sensed a presence behind him, realized it was a grandmother looking at puffy jackets with a kid about Nessa's age. Yeah, they couldn't have this conversation in here. "Come on." He held out his hand to Aileen, realized he was holding his breath until she placed her hand in his.

He guided them out of the store, down the pathway of shops to a quiet spot that overlooked the back half of a marina. Most of the boats, even the obnoxious yachts, had holiday lights strung up in various places.

They sat on one of the benches and he was careful to scan the area. No one could approach them without him seeing them first.

"So," he said. "I'm sorry for my response the other day."

"You mean your rejection?" Her tone was dry.

He blinked, stared at her profile—because she was staring out at the marina instead of meeting his gaze. "I wasn't rejecting you." He could *never* reject her. He cleared his throat. "I was simply taken off guard, that's all."

She snorted softly, as if she didn't believe him.

He shifted an inch closer, wrapped his arm around her shoulders. They'd been so casual with affection before, and even though he'd always wanted more than friendship, he still craved simply touching her. The last couple days without her had been hell. "I could never reject you, Aileen. You're...my best friend." The only best friend he'd ever had, something he was too embarrassed to admit. But she knew everything about him. Or at least the important stuff. And she'd accepted all of him. He never had to worry about acting in front of her. So yeah, her asking him to take her to bed had thrown him because it was everything he'd ever dreamed about. But he knew if he admitted the depths of his feelings, it would scare her.

She made a sort of strangled sound and covered her face with her hands. "Dante!"

He blinked again, unsure what he'd said. "You're not having sex with anyone but me."

She looked up at him in disbelief, dropping her hands to her lap. "What?"

"That's right. You're not hiring someone and you're certainly not having sex with that loser from tonight." Oh, the things he would do to her. Dirty, delicious things he'd only allowed himself to fantasize about.

"He's not a loser."

Dante gritted his teeth. The man was a dead loser. But that was just semantics. "Either way, you want to reclaim that part of yourself and you'll do it with me."

Now she was the one blinking. Once. Twice. Three times... She turned to face the marina. "I don't want you to do it out of pity."

"I'm not." Not even close.

She was quiet a long moment, as though weighing his answer. "So...I don't have much experience."

He mentally fist-pumped the air because she was still talking to him about this, not rejecting the idea she'd originally proposed. "That's okay." He'd been with women before her, but no one after they'd met.

Crossing her arms over her chest, she nibbled on her bottom lip. Her body language was closed off, but he could see the cogs in her brain working. She was thinking about this so he remained very still, not wanting to spook her. Above all, he wanted her to trust him. If this happened between them, he would make damn sure he laid all her fears to rest.

"Okay, say we do this."

Oh, they were. He'd thought of barely anything else the past few days. Years, if he was being honest.

"Then no one knows about it. It's just one friend, doing another friend a favor. I don't want Nessa to find out anything and get confused about...us."

Dante kept his expression relaxed, but screw that. "We'll keep things between us." *For now.* Because it certainly wouldn't be a secret forever. *Nope.*

She breathed out a sigh of relief, letting her arms drop. "Okay, good. And no one else can know either, because you know how my parents are. And...everyone in the neighborhood. I don't want them in our business."

Dante didn't think this was because she was embarrassed of him, but it still stung. He buried those feelings, however, because this was about her. She'd had her choice taken from her long before he'd known her. Then that monster had tried to force her to stay in his life by fighting for custody of Nessa.

He'd paid dearly for his crimes—Dante only wished he'd been the one to kill the guy. Or hell, if he was making wishes, he wished Aileen had never been hurt at all.

But since he couldn't go back in time, he'd do what he could for her now. He wanted her to feel safe, in control. Even if it killed him in the end to have a taste of her then watch her walk away, he'd do anything to make her happy.

CHAPTER 5

The worst lies are the ones we tell ourselves.

"Your cookies are the best, Mom." Nessa looked at Aileen's decorated candy cane cookies, then eyed her own critically and frowned.

"I know you love to compete, but this isn't a competition, my sweet girl." Aileen took one of Nessa's bright pink and neon yellow candy canes and took a bite. "And yours taste delicious."

Nessa grinned and picked up her spoon, scooped up some more of the pink icing and started smearing it on another cookie with absolutely no finesse, this one shaped like a snowflake. They'd been baking and decorating cookies the last couple hours. Well, Aileen had mostly been doing the baking but Nessa had been helping and hanging out. And Aileen was happy Nessa still wanted to be around her mom. Because she knew her time was limited. Nessa was already independent and would soon pull away even more than she already was.

At the sound of the door to the mudroom opening, she glanced up, froze for a moment when she realized it was Dante and her dad stepping inside. She'd invited her mom and dad over and clearly they'd invited Dante. He had on a simple black T-shirt and jeans, but that shirt had been created to mold to his biceps. It stretched across his arms and over his chest, highlighting exactly what kind of shape the man was in—perfect.

"Hey, hon," her dad said as he stepped into the kitchen, looking at the array of cookies with interest. "Brought Dante with me to look at that electrical issue."

"I'll take payment in cookies." Dante's voice was teasing, but there was a hint of something else in his eyes that she felt aaaaall the way to her core.

Oh, she was in so much trouble with him. After their deal or decision or whatever last night, she was only just starting not to freak out when she thought about having sex with him. Because they hadn't really gone into detail about...what or when they were going to get down to business.

And she was embarrassed to admit that it was all she could think about now that he was on board. She was trying to convince herself that this was just transactional (without any kind of actual payment) and nothing more. It was one friend doing another friend a favor.

But she was a liar.

Because he made her feel safe, always had. Which was ridiculous because he was a hitman, but he'd always been so kind to her. Long before she'd been aware of him as a man, he'd simply been her friend. But things had changed over the last few years. She'd been moving past her trauma and was very, very aware of just how masculine Dante was. She'd started to look at him like more than a friend. Waaaay more.

"Thank you both, and yes, all the cookies you want." She leaned into her dad for a hug, then shoved a plate of decorated wreaths at Dante when he rounded the island.

Because apparently she'd decided to kick up the awkward between them by about a hundred notches. It wasn't like he'd come over to her to start making out in front of everyone. But she'd needed a barrier in the form of cookies. Because she had no idea how to have normal sex. Or sex at all. Or how to be intimate with someone who was also her best friend. *Gah!*

"My mom had a date last night," Nessa announced cheerily.

Aileen looked at her daughter, who didn't even glance up from decorating. "Ah, yeah, I did," Aileen said. She hadn't told anyone about running into Dante and Elli, and didn't think Elli had said anything either. Not that she'd heard anyway. And she had no doubt her parents would have said something about her being mugged. They took overprotective to the next level.

She loved Elli so much for her discretion alone. Unlike everyone else in the neighborhood, Elli didn't treat her like she was made of spun glass and she didn't stick her nose into Aileen's business.

"I hope they go on a second date," her daughter continued, oblivious to the tension rolling off Dante.

Her dad was busying perusing the cookies, but then said, "So, how was it?"

"What?" Aileen asked.

"The date?" He snagged one of the snowman cookies, nodded approvingly at it.

"Oh, fine. Ah, I mean, nice. I had cake." *Oh. My. God.* Could she sound more stupid? What was coming out of her mouth right now? *I had cake!* She sounded like she was five. To her credit, it was hard to concentrate when Dante was right there, clearly not liking her talking about her date if his dark expression was any indication.

Maybe it was because of...their deal? But that was just a friend helping a friend out. No...this was just awkward and she was simply getting in her head.

"So where's Mom?" she asked, wanting to talk about anything but her date.

"She was finishing something up for the party, but will be over later." Her dad motioned for Dante to come with him, then the two of them disappeared and moments later she heard their soft footfalls heading up the stairs.

Aileen could suddenly breathe easier without Dante so close—and smelling so good she wanted to bury her face in his neck. While wrapping her body around him and climbing him like a tree. Jesus, she had issues.

"Why'd you tell them I had a date?" she asked when it was just the two of them.

Nessa looked up, her expression almost too innocent. "Was it a secret?"

"No. I was just asking."

"I thought they'd like to know. It's a big deal and I'm happy you're dating."

"Really?" She'd told Nessa that she might try dating, but that she'd never bring anyone home. Of course that would change if she got serious with someone, but she never wanted to lie to her daughter about where she was going so she'd been up front. At this point she couldn't even imagine bringing anyone home to meet her. You know, except Dante. But that was a different can of worms.

"Yeah! Not that I think you need a man, but I want you to be happy."

She wrapped her arm around her daughter, squeezed. "I am happy. I've got you."

"Well duh. But you know what I mean." She jumped off her stool, shoved it back. "Can I go play soccer? Tia's parents set up new nets in their backyard. We'll have a couple hours before the party."

"Sure. Let me just check with her parents." The neighborhood holiday party wasn't for another five hours so they had plenty of time. And her daughter definitely needed to burn off energy.

"They know I'm coming over," Nessa called out as she raced up the stairs, likely to change into her practice gear.

"Of course I'm the last one hearing about it," she murmured to herself as she texted their neighbors and longtime friends.

She received an immediate response telling her to send Nessa over when she was ready. Not long after the front door slammed behind Nessa, Aileen got another text telling her that her daughter had made it safely. So she packed away all the frosted deliciousness then headed up to her office to make a handful of ASMR videos. She tended to make them in batches so she had a buffer of time for uploads, especially around the holidays. And her office's sound insulation was incredible thanks to her parents, who'd installed it themselves years ago. Sure, they were overprotective, but they were also incredibly supportive.

She hoped to see Dante before he left—alone—and make up for the weirdness of shoving a plate of cookies at him.

Seriously, what was wrong with her? No, she knew the answer to that: now that sex was on the table, she'd turned into an anxious lunatic.

By tonight she was going to get it together, because after the holiday party Nessa was staying with her grandparents for the night. It was the perfect time for Aileen and Dante to...explore things. She didn't think she was ready for full-on sex, but she wanted to get naked with another human.

No, not just another human, but Dante. God, she was trying to play this off as just friends, but the truth was he meant everything to her. Had for a long time. He was a constant in her life. And he knew about her past, knew the truth of Nessa's parentage. He knew her inside and out and had been one of her closest confidants. Then she'd tossed a grenade into things and...couldn't even regret it.

She knew she was going to get burned, knew she had to play things cool, especially with someone like him. He'd traveled the world, had so much experience and likely had lovers everywhere. That was the one thing they'd never talked about so she didn't actually know for sure, but she had eyes. The man was built like a god, had an edge to him, and she had no doubt women just flocked to him.

Ugh. That was definitely *not* something she wanted to think about now. Or ever. Barftastic, as Nessa liked to say about anything she found gross.

Great, now she was quoting her eleven-year-old.

Shaking off the thoughts of her chaotic mind, she pulled up her laptop to check emails and social media messages before diving into making videos. She had a virtual assistant who helped with a lot of the back-end stuff, and a great video editor, but she liked to be the one who responded to messages.

Just as she finished reading through all the new or important messages, she frowned at a new message that popped up.

Your last video was clearly rushed. It's a stinking pile of hot garbage. Stick to what your viewers like or you won't like the fallout. Just because you've gotten so big doesn't mean you can forget about your original fans. We made you and we can break you.

A shudder snaked down her spine. It was just words on a screen, she reminded herself as she got ready to make her videos. But she saved it in her "red flag file" just in case she needed it later. It wasn't the first weird message she'd gotten and she knew it wouldn't be the last. But for now she was going to shelve it and deal with it in the future if necessary.

At least that was what she told herself, but she couldn't shake the feeling of unease even hours later as she got ready for the party she'd been looking forward to for ages.

CHAPTER 6

*If you were able to believe in Santa Claus
for eight years, you can believe in yourself
for like five minutes.*

Dante took the small glass mug that Sarah, a former hitman, shoved into his hand. Roughly in her sixties, though it was hard to tell for sure, the dark-haired woman was only happy in December. She'd once told him it was because it was the month her ex-husband had died, not because of the holidays.

Either way, it was the only time of year she ever smiled.

"What's this?" He sniffed it cautiously.

She rolled her eyes. "Christmas punch, dumbass, not poison."

Poison hadn't been her forte anyway, garrotes had been. "Smells good."

"Because it is good. I made it with just the right amounts of champagne, rum, cranberry, cider and just a hint of orange. Perfection," she said on a happy sigh.

"You're in a good mood," he murmured, taking a sip of it, finding it not too sweet. Huh, it actually was good.

"Of course I am. Elli told me you'd be singing tonight and we're all ready for the show."

He froze for a moment, then sighed. "I'd forgotten about that," he muttered before stalking away from her.

Almost everyone from the neighborhood was here at Manuel's house, the biggest one in their neighborhood of hitmen. At five thousand square feet, with a huge pool and lanai area and big sliding glass doors that opened from both the kitchen and attached living room to the outside, this place had been built with entertaining in mind.

As he made his way through the throng of people in the kitchen, Hudson stepped in front of him. "Hey."

Dante blinked. "Hey, didn't know you were coming tonight." Hudson didn't live in the neighborhood with the rest of their professional group, but on a boat in one of the local marinas. He said that being tied down in a static place made him anxious, which Dante could understand.

"Lorna threatened to put my balls in a vise if I didn't." Hudson gave a dry smile.

"Liar. You'd have come anyway."

"Well I *did* hear that you were singing." Hudson grinned. "And that you'd be wearing a costume."

"Man, fuck you," he muttered, glancing around, still trying to find Aileen. He'd been here for half an hour and still hadn't seen her. She'd still been working in her office when he'd left hours ago and he hadn't wanted to disturb her. But after what Nessa had said about her date—and hoping that Aileen went on another one—he was on edge. He needed eyes—and more—on Aileen.

Where the hell was she? The place was spread out, but it wasn't that big and he knew everyone here.

Elliana and Theo appeared out of nowhere, Theo wearing an ugly Christmas sweater and Elliana in a dark green and black sweater with a reindeer carrying TNT.

Theo clapped hands with him and pulled him into a hug.

"Glad to have you back. How was the trip?" Dante asked as he stepped back. He'd missed his friend.

"Good, but I'm glad to be home. I heard you and Elli did a little recon earlier in the week?"

"What recon? What's going on?" Hudson turned back from watching a trio of women singing karaoke.

"No recon, just Christmas shopping," Dante said, taking Elliana by the arm.

No way was he letting Hudson know what he'd been up to. For a hitman, Hudson was surprisingly chatty. "I'm going to steal your wife for a second. Here." He shoved the champagne cider stuff into Theo's hands, then tugged Elliana with him into a quiet-ish corner of the kitchen near a dessert table.

"Look, I was going to tell you after the party. Chill." Elliana held up her hands before she snagged a small plate and started piling on petit fours.

"Tell me what? And where is Aileen?" he murmured, glancing around to make sure no one was listening.

"Oh, I thought that was why... Anyway, I might have found the mugger. I thought that's what you wanted to talk about. And Aileen is over there," she said with a chin nod as she added a blondie to her plate.

"Are you serious?" he asked even as he zeroed in on Aileen, saw her talking to Theo and Hudson.

Was Hudson a little too close to her? Dante frowned, then cursed himself. He needed to get over his shit. Aileen had come to him, not Hudson. And jealousy wasn't going to get him anywhere with her—even if he wanted to create a bubble around her, keep all men at a six-foot radius. At least.

"Yep. He's just some petty thief. I think we should totally pay him a visit to scare him straight but I feel bad for the guy. His mom died when he was sixteen and he's paying for his sister's college."

Dante scrubbed a hand over his face. "He mugged Aileen."

"I know, that's why Theo and I will go with you when you talk to him. To make sure you don't kill him."

"I'm not having this conversation now," he muttered, deciding to end it while he was ahead.

Not saying another word, he stalked across the kitchen toward Aileen, felt that gut punch when she smiled up at him. She was like the sun and he simply wanted to bask in her warmth.

"Elliana wanted to talk to you guys about something," he said to Theo and Hudson, lying straight to their faces so he could get rid of them.

They both headed off as Dante slid closer to Aileen, inhaled her sweet scent.

"Hey, where's the nugget?" he asked, wishing he had the right to pull her into his arms, kiss her senseless—give her orgasm after orgasm. But she wanted to keep their arrangement just between them. Meanwhile, he wanted to stake a claim for everyone they knew.

She wore an emerald green sweater dress that hugged her curves in all the right places and brought out her already captivating eyes. Eyes he would happily drown in. "She's waiting in line to sing karaoke with some of the other kids. My parents are on 'Nessa watch' tonight, said they wanted me to let my hair down for the party."

Sounded about right. "You look amazing," he murmured, pitching his voice low enough for just her.

Her cheeks flushed pink, and going on instinct, he slid his hand into hers. "Come on, let's go somewhere quieter."

Her eyes widened slightly but she fell in step with him as he headed down a hallway, then ducked into what turned out to be a butler's pantry.

Immediately the noise from the party fell away as he shut the door fully behind them and turned the flimsy lock into place.

"Is everything okay?" she asked even as she hopped up onto one of the countertops and slipped her heels off, moaning in what sounded like relief.

He wanted to make her moan under very different circumstances.

Moving slowly, he leaned down and caged her in with his hands, was grateful when she spread her legs to make room for him. He was over being subtle now that she'd told him what she wanted. And they were alone, so no one to see.

He wasn't breaking any dumb rules.

"Should we be doing this?" she whispered even as she slid her hands up his chest, settled them nervously on his shoulders.

"Absolutely we should," he murmured as he dipped his head to hers, capturing her mouth in a gentle kiss when he really wanted to devour her. She already consumed most of his waking thoughts, and he wanted to consume her. With orgasms.

He needed to do things slow for her—but not so slow that she got too into her thoughts and decided to pull away from him. Because he knew her, probably better than she realized.

Her fingers tightened on his shoulders and she pulled him to her instead of pushing away. Good, because he couldn't bear if she pushed him away.

Her kisses were sweet and tentative at first, but when she wrapped her legs around his waist and pulled him closer, he nearly lost it. This was a big deal for Aileen, who'd been in her shell for years. She'd always worn armor where almost everyone was concerned, but she'd started letting him in years ago, letting him be a part of her life.

She moved her hips against him, made little moaning sounds every time his hard length rubbed against her unfortunately covered clit.

Moving slowly, wanting to give her plenty of time to tell him to stop, he slid his hand down her sides then over her thighs before he pushed her dress up to her waist.

She bit his bottom lip as he toyed with the edge of her silky underwear, wondering if he'd lost his mind. He should have waited until they were at her house. Or his.

But screw it. After years of wanting her, she was in his arms now and he wasn't going to ruin this shot for them.

"Is this okay?" he murmured against her mouth even as he slowly cupped her mound. He knew it had been at least eleven years since she'd been intimate with someone so he wanted to be sure.

She sucked in a breath, her eyes dilated as she looked up at him. "Definitely."

"I want you to come on my fingers."

Her cheeks flamed red now, but she still nodded, her breathing unsteady.

"Is that okay?" he asked, pushing a little. "I want you to say it." After everything she'd been through, he wanted to *hear* her consent. Wanted to make sure they were on the same page the entire time, because he'd rather cut off a part of himself before he ever hurt or scared her. Even unintentionally.

"Yes, make me come. I need this." Her words were a bare whisper, but yep, he'd take it.

He kissed her again, claiming her mouth as he teased his finger between her slick folds. Ready for her to realize that this was too fast, he was prepared to pull back if so.

But she spread wider for him, rolling her hips, urging him on, so he slid his finger all the way inside her.

"Dante," she groaned against his mouth.

Hearing her say his name like that, with such need, had him harder than he'd ever been. But he focused on her even as he shifted uncomfortably, and began moving his finger inside her in slow thrusts. "Are you still good?"

"Oh my god, Dante! Yes. Please," she moaned out the last word.

She tightened around him with each explorative push, but when he teased her clit, he *felt* that reaction.

"Oh, god." She jerked against him, her inner walls now clenching almost convulsively around his finger with each tease of her clit, and she was so damn wet.

"Not god, Dante will do just fine." He nipped her bottom lip as he continued pleasuring her.

She let out a strangled laugh-moan. "Faster please. *Please.*"

"You never have to beg me, baby. Never." He slid another finger inside her even as he cupped her breast through her dress. What he wouldn't give to have her stretched out under him, completely naked. *Soon.* "I'll make you come anytime, anywhere."

The material of her bra had to be flimsy because he could feel her hard nipple, pinched, then rolled it oh so gently—and set her off.

Maybe it was the onslaught of pleasure, but she jerked against him as she let out a cry of surprise, coming against his fingers in a climax that seemed to stretch on forever.

Yet it wasn't long enough.

Her hips rolled against his hand, her slickness coating his fingers as her inner walls tightened over and over around them.

As she came down from her high, she blinked up at him, her eyes still a little hazy and wild. "That was amazing," she whispered.

"It was just an appetizer." He claimed her mouth in a slow, lazy kiss even though he was harder than he'd ever been in his life. Because this was Aileen, the only woman for him. "After the party, we can do whatever we want, all night long."

Blinking a little dazedly, she nodded. "All night—"

The door rattled, then suddenly flew open.

Cranky, retired Sarah stood there, eyes wide, mouth open like a stupid fish as she stared at the two of them.

"Shut the door," Dante snarled even as he began tugging Aileen's dress down. He hadn't even gotten to taste her yet. And he knew he'd locked that door. *Damn it.*

Even as Sarah muttered an apology and started to shut the door, Aileen hopped down and raced after her, leaving her shoes behind as she straightened her dress.

"Shit," Dante muttered to the empty room as he picked up her heels. He couldn't run after her with his dick as hard as it was. No hiding his reaction now.

As he started thinking of anything that would get rid of his erection, Aileen ducked back into the room, slightly out of breath. "It's okay, I talked to her and she's not going to tell anyone. Also, apparently this lock doesn't work," she said dryly.

Dante didn't care if Sarah blasted it from the speakers or sang it in a karaoke version, and it hurt more than he wanted to examine that Aileen didn't want anyone to know about them.

At least she wasn't pulling away or acting as if she regretted things. After sliding on her heels, she wrapped her arms around him and held him close. "That was amazing. Thank you."

"You're amazing."

She smiled up at him as if he'd hung the moon, and okay, fine, if she didn't want people to know, he could live with it if she kept looking at him like this.

"You're definitely coming over later tonight," she said as she stepped out of his embrace. "And I'm going to take care of you," she added, a wicked glint in those green eyes.

Oh, hell, his erection was back. "You go first," he rasped out. "I'm going to need a minute." Or an hour.

In a bath of ice.

CHAPTER 7

Dear Santa, just bring coffee. And wine.

"I can't believe you got out of singing tonight." Aileen slid her arms around Dante as he stepped into her kitchen, marveling at how *not* weird it was to be intimate with him.

Okay, it was still a little weird, but the good kind.

It would make things harder once they stopped this whole thing. But he'd been so incredible in that butler's pantry, so patient.

Too patient. Not that she could ever complain about that. He hadn't known her in the direct aftermath of the assault, but he knew about her past. So she appreciated how gentle he was being. And now she needed more from him. Needed to feel totally in control of her life again and that meant not being treated as if she'd break.

Dante grunted, his gaze dipping to her mouth as he pinned her against the countertop. His dark eyes were filled with need, his expression telling her exactly what he wanted to do—and she loved it. This wasn't the sweet and helpful Dante who came over to help out, this was the Dante who was going to bang her brains out. "I'm just glad the party is over."

"Me too..." Trailing off, she frowned as she heard the distinctive alert of her front door opening. *Shit.* She jumped back when she heard her mom calling out.

Dante sighed but she slid out from his hold and headed through the kitchen, surprised to see her mom holding Nessa—who was almost too big to hold anymore. Her daughter had been looking forward to a sleepover all week.

"Princesa isn't feeling well," her mom murmured as she set Nessa on her feet. "She wanted to come home."

Nessa turned to look at her, already in her soccer-themed pajamas, her face pale. "It's my tummy, Mommy."

Uh oh, she only got "mommy" when Nessa was truly sick.

Aileen held out her hand. "Okay, let's—"

Nessa started puking, and before she'd taken a full step, Dante sprang into action. "Come on." He carried her over to the sink where she continued to empty the contents of her stomach.

Wincing, Aileen stepped over the mess and hurried to rub her daughter's back. When it seemed like Nessa was done, she asked, "Are you still feeling like you're going to throw up?"

"I don't know. No, I don't think so." Her voice was raspy, tired as she leaned against the countertop.

Aileen felt Nessa's forehead. Didn't feel hot but she grabbed a digital thermometer anyway and held it up. "No fever, so that's good. What did you eat tonight?" Normally she had a pretty good idea of what her daughter ate but she'd been running around with her friends.

"Cake."

"That doesn't sound too bad." It had been a lot of chocolate-looking stuff that came back up.

"No, like a whole cake. And I drank a bunch of soda." She whispered the last part, probably because she wasn't supposed to have it. "One of my crew bet me I couldn't eat a whole cake," she added, almost a little mutinously. "Proved them wrong."

Aileen bit back a sigh. No wonder her kid was sick. And since when did she have "a crew"? Did she mean her soccer team friends? She'd worry about that later. "Come on, let's get you upstairs and into some fresh clothes—and you can brush your teeth. I think you need sleep more than anything. Mom, you can leave that. I'll get it after she's settled."

"I'll get it, Lorna," Dante said before her mom could answer. "Just go on home. I'll sanitize the kitchen while she takes care of Nessa."

Lorna simply smiled, looking more than a little exhausted. "I won't argue with you about cleaning up puke. Call me if you need anything," she said, looking between the two of them before she headed out.

"Dante, are you sure—"

"Just take care of Nessa," he murmured.

Nodding, she scooped her up, glad she could still hold her, if just barely. Nessa already had some height on her, was all skinny arms and legs now. But as she laid her head on Aileen's shoulder, she soaked this up. Puke breath and all.

"I'm sorry you're sick, baby," she whispered as she took Nessa to the bathroom. "Want me to put toothpaste on your brush?"

Nessa nodded pitifully so Aileen got that ready, then grabbed her some more clothes and returned to the bathroom to find her throwing up in the sink again.

Aileen sighed. It was going to be a long night. And not the kind she'd been planning on.

***

"Hey," Aileen whispered as she stepped into the kitchen. Her spotless kitchen that smelled like lemon and bleach. She'd gotten Nessa to sleep a few hours ago, then had crashed herself. But once the sun was up, she was too. She'd thought Dante would have gone home already. "I thought you left."

Shaking his head, he pulled down a mug, poured her the freshly brewed coffee. "Slept on the couch."

"You could have taken the guest room."

He just shrugged and picked up his own mug.

"I'm sorry last night didn't work out the way we'd hoped," she murmured.

He frowned slightly. "You don't ever have to apologize for that. Nessa comes first."

She smiled at his tone. "Always."

"So how is she?" he asked as he moved to her fridge, started pulling out a carton of eggs.

"Ah...good. Are you cooking?"

"Yep. Sit. Relax, I know you've got to be exhausted."

"I feel like I should protest but I'm not going to," she said on a laugh. "Thank you for cleaning up last night. I know how much that sucks."

He shrugged. "I've cleaned up worse."

She blinked, not quite sure how she should interpret it, then realized she really didn't want to know. She was well aware of what her own family did or had done for a living and she could admit that she compartmentalized some of it. "Well, I appreciate it. She finally dozed off after keeping down some water and crackers. I think she just wreaked havoc on her system with all that sugar and her body rejected it."

"Can't believe she ate a whole cake," he murmured, shaking his head as he started cracking eggs.

"On a dare."

He snorted. "That sounds like her."

"Yep. No one's going to tell her what she can't do," Aileen said on a sigh, already worried about teen Nessa. But that was a problem for future Aileen. "I'm just glad she's okay." She glanced at her phone screen, saw the time. "I was supposed to volunteer today with this toy delivery thing for Christmas, but I think I'm going to have to cancel." Because she knew her parents both had plans today and she was pretty sure Theo wasn't letting Elliana out of the house after being gone the last week.

"Why? I'll watch Nessa." He shrugged as he added a little seasoning and shredded cheese to the scrambled eggs.

"I can't ask you to do that." Not that it would be the first time, but he'd spent the night here cleaning up puke and he couldn't have been comfortable on the couch. She didn't want to take advantage of their friendship, especially when their relationship was on new and unfamiliar territory. He'd always helped out in the past and she'd never thought twice about it, but things were different now.

"You're not actually asking, I'm offering. She'll probably be asleep for a while anyway. I saw it on your calendar," he said, nodding to the one on her fridge. "I'd planned to offer already."

"Oh. Wow, thank you." She hadn't wanted to cancel, not when she'd volunteered months ago.

"Why do you sound so surprised? I've watched her before."

"I know. Things are just...different now, I guess."

He glanced over his shoulder at her and she couldn't quite read his look. It was intense but was that a good thing? Ugh, she hated that she had almost no experience and now she was fooling around with her best friend and...where did that leave them? And of course he looked amazing this morning, as if he'd had a full night of sleep instead of on a cramped couch. His dark hair was a little mussed, but that only added to his sexy vibe.

"Whatever you're thinking about, just stop," he growled.

"You're not even looking at me."

"I can feel your thoughts all the way over here. And the nugget is coming down the stairs. I heard a little thump."

It said a lot for how distracted she was that she hadn't even heard Nessa, but sure enough, her daughter stumbled into the kitchen, her long braid messy, expression grumpy. "I'm hungry," she grumbled. "But not for cake."

Aileen bit back a laugh.

Dante, however, chuckled and Aileen absolutely loved the sound. "I'm cooking scrambled eggs for your mom," he said without turning around. "Is that good or too much for your tummy right now?"

Nessa laid her head on the countertop, still looking a little pathetic. "Ugh."

"I'll make you some toast for now." Aileen kissed the side of her forehead and slid off her stool. "Dante's going to hang out with you for a few hours this morning."

Nessa sat up at that, looking like her normal mischievous daughter. "I can finally slay you in our VR game."

"Or," Aileen said before Dante could respond, "you can relax and watch movies or something equally light while I'm gone. You need rest."

Dante didn't respond, simply plated her food then literally shooed her to sit and took over with the toaster and Nessa's drink as well.

Oooh, no. Aileen had a sort of mental blip as she registered that he was just taking over, being all wonderful. Taking care of both her and Nessa. Everything about right now felt so...normal.

Nice.

No, nice was too bland a word. How about absolutely freaking wonderful? Oh god, she was in all sorts of trouble. Why had she ever thought that just having sex with Dante would be easy? That they could go back to being friends after seeing each other naked. Having orgasms! That she could ever look at him the same after he'd brought her to climax in their neighbor's butler's pantry. *Sweet. Flying. Reindeer.* She hadn't thought any of this through! And now he was in her house, taking over and helping out and making her want way more than orgasms.

"Mom?" Nessa's voice pulled her out of her thoughts.

She blinked, realized she was staring at a fork of scrambled eggs. "Yeah?"

"Are you okay?"

"I'm great." She realized that Dante was now watching her curiously too. "But how are you feeling?"

Nessa shrugged, back to normal apparently now that she'd woken up fully. "Great. Toast is fine, but I need more food."

"I'll cook some eggs for you," Dante said, and Aileen could feel his gaze on her.

So she met his eyes and smiled, though it felt forced. When he started cracking more eggs, she shoveled her food in her mouth, then basically sprinted from the room to get ready—and definitely to escape his watchful, knowing gaze.

CHAPTER 8

I've been dreaming of a white Christmas,
but if it runs out, I'll drink the red.

"Hey," Aileen answered on the second ring when she saw Elli's name on-screen. "You have good timing. I'm just leaving the center."

"How'd the toy drive go?"

"Really good. And on top of the toy donations for the kids, we raised a lot of money for the community center. And, I heard that an anonymous donor pledged to double whatever we brought in today."

"Well, triple if you want to get technical."

She laughed lightly. "I knew it was you, and you're wonderful."

"You're not wrong. So how's my perfect angel doing?"

"Good. Turns out she just made herself sick by eating an entire cake."

Elli snorted. "Oh my god, what was she thinking?"

"Your perfect angel is eleven, Elli. She *wasn't* thinking." Aileen fished out her car keys as she reached her car. Dark clouds had rolled in an hour ago, but luckily no rain yet. "Actually, she was determined to prove someone wrong."

"That's my girl."

"I swear to god—" Aileen let out a short scream as another freaking Santa raced out from behind the row of cars, a pistol in his hand.

"Toss your keys to me, then give me your purse," he snarled.

"Aileen, what's going on?"

"And your phone."

Time seemed to slow as she stared into the dark, angry eyes of the poorly dressed Santa. She didn't think it was the same guy as the other night because he seemed shorter but she'd been sitting then. And it had happened so fast.

"Can you hear me?" he snarled again, stalking closer, waving his pistol around her face. "Give me your keys and get in your car! We're going for a ride."

Oh, no, no, no. She wasn't getting in her car with him.

When she didn't move fast enough, he lunged for her, his gun arcing downward—and away from her.

And in that moment, her parents' and Theo's training kicked in. She swung up hard with her purse, knocking the pistol out of his hand.

It clattered to the concrete, falling under her car.

He cried out in surprise, but he wasn't stunned for long. As he dove for it, she turned and sprinted back toward the community center. There were two cops working the event, and while normally she was the last person to involve law enforcement, desperate times and all that.

She screamed as she ran, hoping to draw attention, and that was when she realized she was still clutching her phone, could hear Elli shouting for her.

Right before she rounded the corner of the building, she glanced over her shoulder, saw the Santa running down the street in the opposite direction.

"Another Santa attacked me," she gasped out as she held her phone up to her ear. "And I've gotta talk to the cops." Words she'd never thought to say. "I'm fine, but I'll call you back." She ended the call, raced up to the nearest police officer.

In khakis, a black polo with the Miami PD logo, he turned, smiling warmly at her. "Aileen, you're back."

"A man dressed as Santa just tried to carjack me." And she was pretty sure there was more to it than that. Because no way two Santas had tried to mug her that close together. Right?

Unless there was some weird Santa crime spree she just hadn't heard about. No way, that would have been splashed across the news so this was something else.

Once the cops jumped into action, everything was a bit of a blur. Even driving to the station to make an official statement, which luckily was only five minutes down the road. Even with traffic. She ignored Elli's multiple calls, then Dante's (she felt bad about that), and then yes, Theo's.

Because she couldn't deal with questions right now. She group texted them that she was fine and would be home soon and that they all needed to chill and not say one single word to anyone yet. Including her parents—especially her parents.

We're going to talk about this later, was Dante's response in a separate text. For some reason she pictured him saying that to her in a really stern brunch daddy voice and she almost caved and called him back.

Because she liked that way too much, she thought as she made her way down to the lobby of the PD substation.

But she couldn't let the three of them just take over like she would have in the past. In addition to trying to take back her sexuality, she wanted to take back all of herself. Her control, her sense of self. And that meant she had to deal with shit on her own, with no one else involved.

Weirdly, today had actually helped. When that asshole had tried to carjack her, likely wanted more than just her car, she hadn't panicked. She'd reacted and then run to safety.

She'd saved herself. And yeah, she knew it could have ended a lot differently, but—

"Crap," she muttered to herself when she stepped into the lobby, saw both her parents sitting there waiting—looking a whole lot like they were planning a murder.

CHAPTER 9

Dear Santa, I can explain...

Dante eyed the rundown apartment complex as they drove slowly through the parking lot, wondering if his target was home.

"You need to calm down," Elli said as she pulled into a parking spot near the apartment they were about to break into.

"I haven't said one single word," Dante bit out even as he tried to temper his rage. He knew she was talking to him and not Theo, even though Theo was in the front seat with her.

Because someone had tried to hurt Aileen. Again.

And he hadn't been there, so he was feeling extra murderous tonight.

Realistically he knew this wasn't his fault, but at the end of the day it didn't matter. Anything could have happened to her. And he couldn't stand the thought of someone hurting her, of the world without her. She'd been through enough and he refused to let the world hurt her again.

She'd brushed all of them off after the attack, told them she was fine. Even *him*. It sliced deep that she hadn't wanted his help.

"That's what worries me," Elli muttered as she turned the engine off.

"You need to stay here and keep watch," Theo said into the quiet as Dante double-checked his weapon and mask.

"What? Why?" Elliana demanded. "I already disabled the complex's security system. It was literal child's play."

"Because there could be any number of doorbell cameras we don't know about. Or other personal security cameras. Or people and their damn phones. Dante and I are used to this and we'll be able to blend in. You, however, are a tall, hot blonde who stands out anywhere, and the only one in this car that *Time* did a spread on. You can't risk being seen and caught on cameras."

"I really hate it when you're logical," she muttered, but she still kissed him then turned to Dante. "You better not do anything stupid, because I guarantee Aileen wants you back whole and unharmed. Be smart!"

He blinked, surprised by her words, but he slid out of the vehicle, tugged his ball cap on low and shut the door.

It was time to take care of business. He was only surprised this place even had a security system. At one time it had been decent, but years of neglect had made the small complex a faded, peeling green, and some of the roofs had long-faded blue tarps that he guessed weren't from the last hurricane but the one before.

Theo strode off in a different direction as Dante headed for the stairs. They'd parked close to their target's apartment, which was on the second floor. Elliana had disabled the system and it was after dark, so that was a plus because there was only one flickering light as he made his way up the sturdy concrete steps.

This place might be falling apart, but it had been built well once upon a time, in the seventies if he had to guess. So the bones of it were solid. Probably why it was still hanging on. If the rest of the place had been built with concrete, there'd be decent insulation. Always a good thing in his line of business.

At the top of the stairs, Theo was waiting across the way at the top of the other set. He shook his head, the code that he hadn't seen anyone to worry about.

Dante removed his ball cap and slid on his thin balaclava while Theo did the same. Then the weapons came out.

Instead of kicking in the door like he wanted to, only because he wanted to bash something in, he picked the lock in less than ten seconds. The door was steel, but the lock was a piece of shit.

Pistol in hand, he eased the front door open and was greeted with a wave of Christmas music. Okay, not what he was expecting. But it confirmed the insulation was good because he hadn't heard it outside.

He motioned to Theo that he was going in first. His longtime friend and sometimes partner on jobs nodded, fell in behind him and closed and relocked the front door.

Adrenaline pumping, Dante moved past a dark room, swept inside. The Christmas music shifted to voices talking and it took a moment to realize it was from a well-known holiday movie.

The first room was a simple bedroom with a twin sized bed, a pink and white comforter and a bunch of moving boxes stacked in one corner.

Theo swept what turned out to be a bathroom in a similar condition—clean and sparse.

They found the man they were looking for in his living room, eating pizza, the TV on low. Adam Jackson, per the info Elliana had dug up. When Jackson saw them, he dropped the piece onto a plate, made a move to get up, but both Theo and Dante had their weapons trained on him.

"Where's the purse you stole the other night when you were dressed like Santa?"

The man swallowed, his hands spread, palms out as he looked between the two of them. Dante knew they looked scary as fuck in their masks, let alone with their weapons—which had suppressors on the ends.

"Don't even think about lying," Dante growled, when it seemed the guy might. Because he had zero tolerance for bullshit or wasted time right now. He knew Theo didn't want to kill the guy, but Dante had no such compunction.

"In the first bedroom, in the closet. Top shelf behind a pair of jeans," the man blurted, his dark eyes darting back and forth between them.

"You check," Dante said. "If it's a trap, I'll shoot him in the knee."

Theo kept his weapon up as he left the room, then moments later he came back, held up the dark purple leather handbag. Or clutch. Whatever. "This it?"

"Yep," Dante bit out. "Why'd you attack that woman twice? And why dressed like Santa?" He had a feeling the Santa was just a good cover, but wanted clarification—before he beat the shit out of this guy.

The man blinked, frowning. "I didn't attack anyone. I mean, I pushed that woman when I took her handbag," he said, chin nodding to the purse Theo had set down on a nearby table.

Dante had to rein in his rage as he found his voice.

But Jackson continued. "Some guy hired me to take the purse," he added, looking down slightly, having the decency to appear ashamed. "I didn't want to hurt her..."

"Yet you attacked her again today?"

The man's gaze shot up and he was already shaking his head. "I didn't do anything to anyone today! I was with my si—" He clamped his jaw shut.

"Were you going to say sister?" Dante growled, taking a small step forward. "Because we already know about her."

The guy lunged to his feet, rage flaring in his dark eyes.

"Sit," Dante snapped out, the word whiplash sharp. "We're not hurting her. We don't hurt women," he added, his tone pointed.

The man slowly returned to his seat.

"Hands where we can see them," Theo said quietly when Jackson started to lower his arms.

The guy froze, but nodded. "I didn't hurt anyone. And I haven't...done anything like the other night in a while. But it was too much money to pass up and I just lost my job," he muttered. "Cutbacks. Right before Christmas," he added bitterly.

"Who hired you?" Dante demanded, not liking the sound of this at all. It had been planned, intentional. "And why her?"

"I don't know why her, I swear. And I don't know who hired me either, not really. It was a friend of a friend type of thing, asked if I wanted to make some quick cash with a snatch and grab. Said I could keep whatever was in the purse and the purse itself. I just had to turn over the cell phone."

Okay, now they were getting somewhere.

"Why?" Dante pushed.

"I don't know and I didn't ask either."

"Where were you today?" Theo interjected when Dante went to ask another question. "You said you were with your sister."

The guy cleared his throat, nodded as he glanced at a small picture frame of him and a pretty, dark-haired, smiling woman, her arm around him. His expression softened slightly. "We went to the movies, then to a couple shops she wanted to stop at. Then there was a free show on the green near her college. Some holiday thing. She didn't want to go alone, so..." He shrugged, the action jerky.

And damn it, Dante was pretty sure the guy was telling the truth. He looked at Theo, who nodded slightly. They weren't at square one exactly, but this wasn't ideal. They'd been hoping to wrap this up tonight but now they had more questions than answers. Who wanted Aileen's phone, and why?

He looked back at the man. "Tell me the names of the places you stopped at with relative times." Once the guy answered, Dante made it clear they'd be checking his alibi, then continued, "Who is the friend of a friend who contacted you, and how did they contact you? I want their phone number."

"I ran into him at the corner shop. Chance thing. Or...I assume it was. I was just grabbing milk and ran into him in the parking lot. He approached me with the offer and I said yes. Apparently whoever hired him wanted a lot of degrees of separation." He shrugged, but Dante could see the fear in his gaze.

"How do you know the guy?"

"We used to run in the same gang. Feels like a lifetime ago," he murmured, looking down again.

From what they had on him, Dante figured he was being truthful. The man had run in a gang when he'd been a teen, but when his parents died and he started taking care of his sister, he moved them to a different part of Miami and started working a couple shitty, low-paying jobs. He'd been seventeen then and he'd definitely pulled some shady shit too, because he'd been brought in on suspicion of burglary a few times over the years but nothing had ever stuck.

"Had you seen your friend at that gas station before?" Dante asked.

Jackson paused, then shook his head and cursed. "No. So I guess it wasn't a coincidence. He made it clear that he asked me because I don't have a link to him or my old crew anymore so...yeah, that tracks."

"I want his name, his cell phone number and any other gang associations he might have."

Jackson paused, looked between Theo and Dante.

To Dante's surprise, Theo lowered his weapon. "No one will ever know you spoke to us. And I know right now you're contemplating your odds of getting out of here alive if you do tell us the truth. So I'm going to make you an offer I don't think you'll refuse. Because what's going on here is way bigger than you. Our employer is going to offer up a scholarship for your sister, no strings attached. No grade requirements, not that it matters because we know she makes all As and will one day hopefully make a fine doctor. You tell us everything we want to know, we let you walk out of here and your sister gets the rest of her college paid off. Tuition, books, dorm room, everything."

The man blinked, staring at them as if waiting for a punch line.

Dante was surprised by Theo's offer, but kept his expression neutral—not that Jackson could see more than Dante's eyes through the mask.

"I understand why you'd be hesitant to believe us," Theo continued when he didn't respond. With one gloved hand, Theo pulled out a roll of hundred-dollar bills. "And here's some cash to tide you over through the holidays until you can get back on your feet. But there is one contingency—you can't tell anyone about us or that we were here. Nothing about the scholarship, which will be an anonymous donation and have no link to you. Absolutely nothing. Not even a peep to someone you're sleeping with. And we'll know if you talk," Theo growled. "And we also require that you reach out to us if any of your old crew makes contact about any kind of job. I don't care if you think they're not related, we want to know if any of them contact you."

Jackson slowly nodded. "I figure I have a fifty-fifty chance of you guys telling the truth or just shooting me." Then he relayed the name of the man who'd approached him, his last known phone number and the guy's stomping grounds. Which lined up with the guy's history.

"What about today? Do you know who the Santa was today?" Dante asked.

"I don't know anything about that," Jackson said, shaking his head. "I took a one-and-done job so I could pay for my sister's tuition next semester, that's it. And I made it clear that I wouldn't be using a weapon or hurting anyone. I just want my sister to have a better life. And she has no idea about my...extracurricular activities."

"And she won't. Not by us anyway, because we don't exist," Dante murmured now that they'd gotten all they could. He'd have preferred violence, but Theo had a way with getting people to talk.

And hell, this had been the right move. While it might temporarily make Dante feel better to smash the guy's face in, he just looked young and beat down by life as he sat on that couch. And it was clear he loved his younger sister, which was a point in his favor. So if they truly paid for his sister's tuition, he'd be more likely to be honest with them from this point forward.

"You don't exist," Jackson repeated, nodding at them.

Theo left the number of a burner phone that Jackson could call if he heard from his old crew again, but Dante didn't think anything would come of it. This guy had been essentially a throwaway, someone that if ever hunted down wouldn't know enough to cause trouble.

Or at least that was what whoever had hired him thought.

Because they had enough useful information to dig deeper. Someone had asked his old gang for a favor so now they had a starting point.

Once they were in the SUV with Elliana steering out of the place, Dante spoke. "That was smart, what you did back there."

"I know." Theo sounded smug about it.

Dante sighed, silently impressed. "You're so obnoxious."

"True, but it's hard not to be when I'm always right."

Elliana snorted, but Dante could see her grinning from his angle.

"Are you really going to pay for his sister's college?" he continued.

"Yep," Elliana added. "Theo and I talked about it before we picked you up. I knew you'd disapprove, or at least strongly push back, so we didn't tell you."

She wasn't wrong—because he wasn't always rational when it came to Aileen—so Dante didn't argue. All he said was, "Take me to Aileen."

Theo and Elliana exchanged a look that he couldn't quite make out from the front seat, but it felt charged.

Laying his head back on the rest, he ignored them.

CHAPTER 10

Don't get your tinsel in a tangle!

Dante finally allowed himself a measure of relief as he stepped into Aileen's kitchen to find her there with both her parents—who were worried, even if they were hiding it well. But he could see banked anger in their eyes. Someone had targeted their daughter twice and they would pay.

"Is everything handled?" Lorna asked the moment the three of them shut the mudroom door behind them.

"Where's Nessa?" Dante asked before answering.

"At Tia's for the night. Having a sleepover," Aileen said.

Dante nodded, some of his tension easing. Even if he'd rather have Nessa under this roof, Tia's parents were skilled operators. She was safe. "Everything's handled. Theo..." He glanced at his friend, their son... "Handled everything in the best way possible." While Dante wanted to just smash things, Theo had been thinking a lot more clearly and now they had a lead. Plus a slim connection to whoever had hired this guy. It wasn't much, but he'd found out more on less when looking for a target.

Theo shook his head as he kissed the top of Aileen's head. "Nah, it was a team effort. And we got all the information we needed. The guy from the other night isn't the same Santa from today."

"I could have told you that," Aileen murmured as her brother stepped back.

Wearing an oversized, soft-looking green sweater that said *Merry and Bright* on the front, she was sitting at the island top, a mug of what looked like hot cocoa in front of her. No steam coming off it though, so Dante had a feeling it had been sitting there a while.

He wished he could pull her into his arms right now, that they weren't hiding what they were—whatever that was—from everyone. Hell, maybe he needed some comfort now too. He could have lost her today.

She shrugged when everyone looked at her, but met Dante's gaze. "The man from today was a little shorter and it was a different Santa costume. Not as well made, a little grungier. And...the guy today seemed angrier." She shrugged.

"Are you really okay?" Dante asked, because she'd basically ignored all their texts, saying she was "fine."

She nodded, looking exhausted. "I'm good-ish."

He wished he could kiss her, comfort her, but they weren't... They weren't anything other than best friends who'd fooled around. Once. And in that moment, he hated everything about their agreement.

"We have a small lead," Elliana said. "Thanks to Dante."

Dante frowned, wondering why she was giving him any of the credit.

She didn't look at him as she continued. "The man who robbed you when you were on your date was hired to take your purse, specifically your phone. And it was from an old contact—someone the mugger used to run with. But he's mostly distanced himself from his old life, and the guy who asked him for this told him he could keep the purse and any cash inside." Elliana relayed the rest of the info, including the gang member who'd hired Jackson.

Aileen blinked in surprise. "Did he say why?"

"He didn't know much other than that," Theo said.

"This might not be related, but...Henry and Edith Dupont are in town," Lorna said carefully, her gaze on her daughter.

Aileen stared at her mom for a long moment. "Do you know why?"

It took Dante a full second to realize who Lorna was referring to—the parents of Aileen's now dead rapist. After his life had come to a not-so-tragic end, they'd thought to push for "grandparents' rights" to Nessa. That hadn't lasted long after a visit from Lorna and Nestor that involved arson and destruction of property. No veiled threats from them; they'd been very explicit about what would happen if anyone ever contacted Aileen again. All contact had ceased in the last eleven years.

"Some yearly charity event tomorrow night. They've never gone before, according to our records, but one of their neighbors who has a home here appears to have invited them. I don't know if it's a coincidence that they're here and this is happening or not. I also can't imagine why they'd want your phone."

"How long have you known they were in town?" Aileen asked tightly.

It was clear the question surprised Lorna.

"Only a couple days," Nestor murmured before Lorna could respond. "We didn't say anything because we didn't want to ruin your holidays."

Aileen simply nodded, but her expression was still tight, worried. "I can't imagine why someone would want my phone. And I've never even heard of that gang, so no connection there. But I am going to that charity gala."

Once again, everyone looked at her in surprise. Including Dante.

"With who?" he more or less demanded, impressed by his own restraint. When the hell had this been decided? And who the hell was she going with? The thing was tomorrow night and she hadn't said anything.

Her cheeks flushed as she lifted a shoulder. "Diego, from the other night."

"Who is this man, and how did you meet him?" Nestor demanded before Dante could. "I thought this was just one date, but if it's getting more serious, we need more details on this man."

"Yes, we need to vet him," Lorna added. "He could be behind all this. I didn't realize you had a second date planned or we'd have been more insistent."

To Dante's surprise, Theo didn't look as angry as his parents. Nope, he simply looked at his wife expectantly.

"Diego is fine," Elliana said over the grumbling from her parents. "I used to serve with him. He's not behind any of this. He's my friend and someone I have literally trusted with my life. But I'm going to look more into this angle, dig into the Duponts as well as the guy who hired Aileen's mugger. In fact, I think we need to give her a little space. She's had a long day and needs to rest."

Oh, Dante wasn't going anywhere. "I'll be staying here tonight for security, but first we're talking," he said to Elliana as he stalked from the room.

He didn't wait for a response, and to his surprise, she followed him with no complaint.

Thankfully Theo remained with the others, but Dante wasn't going to tone down this conversation either way. "What the hell, Elliana?" he demanded as the front door shut behind them. He'd known that she was weirdly competitive, but still. It...kind of hurt that she'd set Aileen up with someone, then pretended to do recon with him. She drove him crazy, but he'd thought they might be becoming, ugh...friends.

Around them all of Aileen's lights and blow-up decorations were in full swing, the reds, greens and blues flashing around them on the porch.

"Come on. Away from all this." She chin nodded to the doorbell camera.

Which he'd have thought about if he wasn't so messed up in the head right now. Something that only happened when Aileen was involved.

"You set her up on that date?" he finally snapped when they were on the sidewalk, out of earshot from the cameras. Luckily none of their neighbors were out to see or overhear. "And then went with me to stalk her date? Do you really hate me that much? Is this all a joke to you?" Because he was in love with Aileen and the thought of her with another man was killing him.

Elliana blinked in surprise. "I don't hate you. And I *am* helping you, dumbass! It was taking you *forever* to make a move—both of you. So I figured I'd help things along by setting her up with someone kind and handsome—and loaded. I knew you wouldn't stand for that and I thought you'd finally—finally!—make your move. Which you did, so you're welcome." She folded her arms, looking positively smug.

He stared at her for a moment, unsure what to say. "You set her up because you really want us to get together?"

"Uh, yeah. I absolutely adore Aileen and want her and Nessa to have everything wonderful in the world. They deserve everything they want. And for some reason, that includes you."

Now he was the one blinking in surprise. But before he could respond, Theo, Nestor and Lorna walked out the front door.

"Her parents don't know anything about my plan, so zip it." Elliana mimed a zipper across her mouth, then looked at Theo, her expression softening. "Let's head home and start researching. We're going to find out who wants to hurt Aileen and destroy them. Dante, you talk to her more, try to look at a work angle. That seems like a slim possibility, but push anyway. We're clearly still missing something."

Lorna and Nestor only paused long enough for Lorna to say, "Keep her safe tonight, Dante. Do *not* leave her house. We'll be back in the morning." They headed off with Theo and Elliana, clearly not going to their own home.

Like he was actually going to leave? He just grunted as he headed back up the walk, then shut and locked the door behind him. He found Aileen still in her kitchen, sitting there with her likely now room temperature cocoa in front of her.

"You don't have to stay the night," she murmured, looking beyond exhausted.

"Have you eaten anything?" he asked instead of arguing. He was angry that she'd ignored his texts earlier and that she was apparently going on another date with that kind, loaded guy tomorrow night. Stupid, lucky asshole.

"Are you just ignoring me, then?"

"Kind of how you ignored my texts before?" he asked as he opened her fridge, found enough leftovers to heat up.

She pushed back her stool and headed to the sink, poured out her drink. "I was dealing with the cops and it was hard to text. Or talk on the phone. I just wanted to handle things and get home."

"You shouldn't have been alone." He held up one of her containers of home-made tamales. "This sound good?"

Sighing, she nodded and poured a glass of water before sitting back at the island. "Have you eaten? If not, heat up enough for both of us."

He was too keyed up to eat so he just heated up a plate for her. "I'm assuming the cops were useless, but what did they say?"

She gave him a slightly chastising look. "They were fine. There have been a handful of 'Santa robberies' but no muggings, so I'm not hopeful they'll find out anything. I bet Elli does though."

"Can you think of why anyone would want your phone?" It felt so random, but he knew it couldn't be. Not when she'd been targeted so specifically.

"No... I mean, I've got a ton of pictures of Nessa on them and some of my work stuff saved, but not much."

"What kind of work stuff?"

"Just videos, mostly. And some design stuff, but I tend to do that on my laptop. The videos are outdoor ASMR stuff. It's hard to do them in public though so I have like five. And two I can't use because a couple people got in the shot." She shrugged. "I doubt anyone but me or our family wants my four billion pictures of Nessa playing soccer."

"Maybe it's something you captured at one of her practices," he said as he pulled the plate out. "Feels like a reach, but..." He shrugged. Stranger things had happened. And Nessa's practice was at a public community center with a bunch of soccer fields and basketball courts. They were open to anyone.

"Maybe, but all my stuff is backed up anyway."

He put the hot food and then a small side salad in front of her, still stung that she hadn't reached out to him for help. That she hadn't trusted him enough. "Eat."

She raised an eyebrow but picked up her fork. "Look, I'm sorry I didn't answer your call. I just wanted to handle things on my own. You wouldn't have called anyone so I don't know why it's a big deal that I took care of things."

He paused at her words, starting to understand where she was coming from. "It's not a big deal that you did. I just *wanted* to be there for you, that's all. I know you can handle shit on your own, that's not a question. You're an amazing woman."

"Oh." She watched him for a moment, her cheeks flushing pink as she nodded. "Okay, then."

"But you're not going on that date tomorrow," he growled when what he'd *meant* to say was something a whole lot smoother. He'd meant to ask her not to go, but that ship had now sailed.

She blinked at him, her green eyes wide. "What?"

"No. Date." Oh yeah, that was so much better. He should just start beating his chest at this point. What the hell was wrong with him?

Oh, right—Aileen planning another date with some asshole. Nope, wasn't happening.

CHaPTer 11

An orgasm a day keeps the worries away.

Aileen stared at Dante for a moment, waiting for him to continue, but nope, apparently *no date* was all she was getting. "I didn't hear a request or question in there," she murmured as she took a bite of salad. The truth was, she'd said yes before things between her and Dante had shifted. And she'd only agreed to go platonically. It wasn't like it was a real date.

"I wasn't asking." He pulled a beer out of her fridge and sat across from her, his expression almost challenging.

And ooohhh, she liked this side of Dante. Was this him being...jealous? "What's going on with you?" Her lack of experience was vast and she wanted him to clarify exactly what his whole attitude was about. She was pretty sure she understood, but still, this mattered to her on the most fundamental level.

Because this was Dante.

He pushed up from his seat and stalked around the island, looking a little like he wanted to devour her. After last night—was it just last night?—she was very much okay with that.

"I don't share, Aileen," he murmured as he leaned down, so slowly it was as if time stopped.

The pulse point at her neck was going wild as he moved in. And when he claimed her mouth with a hunger that surprised her, everything else faded away.

Forget food, she simply wanted him. Especially this possessive Dante.

She hadn't even known this type of attitude would be a turn-on for her, but she liked that he didn't want to share, that he was bothered by the thought of her out with another man. Because she couldn't even stomach the thought of him with someone else.

Before she realized what he intended, he had her off the stool and onto the countertop to better match his height. He pushed the plates away and she spread her legs automatically, welcoming him against her. With him she always felt safe, and that in itself was terrifying. She didn't want to get used to this, to having him around, even as she wanted him with what might be considered obsession.

She slid her hands behind his neck as he teased his tongue against hers in a way that made her wonder what it would feel like for him to do the same thing between her legs.

Something she'd been fantasizing about for longer than she wanted to admit. She'd been traumatized when she was in college, but it had been so many years since anyone had touched her intimately and she was at the point where she wanted to crawl out of her skin with need for Dante. For him to touch her exactly like she'd been dreaming about.

Wanting to touch him too, especially after he'd given her a climax last night, she slid her hands down the front of his dark shirt, then up under it, skating her fingertips over all that hardness.

He shuddered under her touch, making her smile against his mouth. She loved that she had that effect on him, that he clearly wanted her as much as she wanted him. This might be about two friends getting intimate but right now she knew this wasn't some pity thing.

He *wanted* her physically. No denying it.

"I want to touch you here," she whispered, sliding one hand between his legs to... Oh, he was reaaally hard. Harder than she'd realized.

"I want to taste you first." A soft demand that came out hungry, desperate.

Heat bloomed inside her at his tone, his need. And she understood because she was right there with him. Her nipples tightened at the thought of one of her fantasies coming to reality but she tensed because he'd be right down there, his face between her legs.

"I've never..." She didn't want to say it, hated admitting how little experience she'd had before everything had gone to shit. But she'd grown up relatively sheltered, and forget about dating before college.

"Do you want me to go down on you?" He was so close, looking right into her eyes, his dark gaze mesmerizing, addicting. And as he asked he slowly slid his hands up under the back of her sweater, palming her bare back with his large, callused hands. Holding her, *anchoring* her.

God, she loved the feel of him touching her, stroking her. And at that thought, she remembered how he'd slid his thick fingers inside her, bringing her to a sharp orgasm.

She nodded, even as insecurities bubbled up. She was trying to take back her control and that meant breaking out of her comfort zone. She trusted Dante to treat her right.

"Say it," he demanded softly. "I want to hear the words."

"I want you to go down on me." Okay she could only get out a whisper, but she'd said it.

His pupils flared, but he didn't waste any time scooping her up off the countertop and carrying her to the living room. "For the record, I want to taste you anywhere, including on the kitchen countertop, but I want you comfortable this first time."

First time? Oh, oh yes, please. *First* implied there would be more. And she wanted to experience everything with him.

That nagging little voice in the back of her head played up on all her doubts, but she silenced it as he slid her pants and panties off with ease.

She leaned back on the couch, wondering about the logistics of this. Should she lie flat or—

"Just lean back and spread your legs." Another soft demand, this one raspier, more desperate. "And..." He grasped the hem of her sweater and lifted up.

She wasn't wearing anything underneath so her nipples beaded even harder under his gaze and the rush of air.

"I wish I had two mouths and four hands," he murmured even as he placed his palms against her inner thighs, pushed gently.

She should feel vulnerable, but in that moment, she felt powerful. Especially when he groaned as he spread her folds with his thumbs, stared between her legs as if she was everything he'd ever dreamed of.

She knew she was letting herself get carried away, but whatever. This was finally happening and she was going to enjoy every single second. For however long things lasted between them.

"You're so perfect," he murmured, his gaze right between her legs.

And yep, that had her feeling all sorts of things. Her inner walls clenched and her clit pulsed at his declaration, because apparently she liked praise.

Slowly, he ran his thumb along her folds, his eyes holding hers right as she sucked in a gasp.

"Perfect," he murmured again. "You were made to be worshipped, baby."

Heat flared inside her, pushing out to all her nerve endings, making it hard to breathe. How was she supposed to keep things compartmentalized when he was looking at her like she hung the moon? And saying things like this?

"When do you take off your clothes?" Because she wanted to see him too.

He blinked, then gave her a slow, wicked grin before he eased back and stripped off his shirt in what could only be described as slow motion.

It was like he was taking his time for her enjoyment and she was so okay with that. Still crouched in front of her, she took in all of him, every hard line and striation, the random scars that seemed to be everywhere. Some more faded than others.

Reaching out, she ran her finger along the scar slicing through his left clavicle. As she did, he slid a finger inside her and she forgot to breathe.

She arched into the slow thrust, clutching onto his shoulder as he buried his finger deep. Then another. Then she forgot to think as he knelt between her legs and began teasing her clit with such enthusiasm, she lost all sense of insecurity. God, his mouth was wicked and perfect and oh...it wasn't going to take her long at all.

It was impossible to be insecure when he was bringing her so much pleasure and growling things like "such a perfect pussy" as he thrust his fingers inside her—as he sucked on her clit. She clutched his shoulders, glad he'd bared some of himself to her at least.

His words set something on fire inside her and when he sucked on her clit again, she completely lost control, coming around his fingers and against his face as he kept stroking her, teasing her and, oh god, her climax just kept going until she was a mess of nerves against the couch.

She gasped as he slowly pulled his fingers from her—then gasped again when he slid them into his mouth.

She stared as he tasted her again, and that rush of heat at seeing him like this helped her shed any inhibitions she might have been holding on to.

She reached for his pants, knowing exactly what she wanted—and hoping he wanted it too. He took over, shoving his pants down, but not fully off, to her disappointment.

"Touch me," he demanded, and without thought she wrapped her hand around his hard length. This was a first for her and she was glad it was with him, that she hadn't gone to a "professional."

He closed his hand around hers, showing her exactly how hard he liked to be stroked. She was surprised by how intensely he stroked himself, but loved that he was being so open with her. And the growly sounds he was making? The dark, hungry expression? Oh god. Yes, please to all of it.

As she continued stroking him, he claimed her mouth, only pulling back when it was clear he couldn't hold on to his control anymore. When he finally came all over her stomach and spread thighs, to her surprise, he rubbed himself into her, looking ridiculously satisfied before he kissed her again, this time softer, sweeter, even as he cupped her breasts. He slowly teased her nipples as he took his time with her mouth and she thought she might combust again from the pure pleasure of him.

"So no gala tomorrow," he murmured against her mouth into the quiet.

She blinked up at him, slightly narrowing her eyes at the surprising topic. "Are you telling me what to do?"

"No, just telling you what's *not* happening." His half grin did all sorts of things to her insides.

It was impossible to be annoyed at him when she was still basking in that orgasm and he was looking at her as if he'd slay dragons for her. "You're ridiculous, Dante." She bit his bottom lip, hoping they weren't done.

But he pulled back slightly then slid his T-shirt over her head. "You need to eat, then we're talking."

"I don't want to talk," she grumbled, but she stood with him. Talking was overrated—she wanted to stay naked. And she definitely wanted more orgasms.

CHAPTER 12

*Sweet, but twisted. Does that make me a
candy cane?*

Sitting in Elliana and Theo's living room, Aileen looked between all the people she loved—arguing about her safety.

As if she wasn't sitting there at all. As if she was a lovely piece of furniture taking up space.

"This is not up for discussion, Dante. She will stay with us until we figure things out. And she will not be going to that gala tonight," her mom snapped after Dante dared to say that she would be safe with him.

"Do I get a say in this?" Aileen asked, her tone dry. Last night her parents had tried to tell her she wasn't going to the gala tonight (and so had Dante) but there could be a benefit to her going. One she needed to talk to them about.

When five pairs of eyes turned her way, she kept her focus on her mom—the real bulldozer. "Because I like the idea of staying at Dante's. Nessa can stay with us too."

Her mom gritted her teeth, but her dad placed a gentle hand on her shoulder, squeezed.

"Maybe Nessa stays with us?" her dad asked in that quiet way of his. "She has a room there already and we'd planned on a couple Christmas activities." Then he motioned to Aileen that it would get her mom off her back if she agreed.

Her mom looked over her shoulder at him. "What was that?"

"Nothing, love." Then he kissed the top of her head.

"Fine, Nessa can stay with you. I can't imagine she has an issue with that. And she doesn't have any more practices until after the New Year, so nothing will seem off to her," Aileen said. Because she didn't want her daughter privy to any of this mess. "Now let's please hear what Elliana has to say." She gave her sister-in-law a beseeching look, hoping she'd get things back on track.

As always, Elliana took over smoothly. "I can't get a clear image of that second Santa from any nearby cameras—because there weren't many. And the cops have found nothing on him so far. Theo and I have been scanning Aileen's photos and pictures—and her ASMR videos online. Nothing is pinging. A couple emails from weirdos, a few trolling comments, but all really generic and from around the globe. None of the trolling comments are local. And the commenters leave the same crap on other creators so it doesn't feel targeted. Even that recent nasty email you got," she added, looking at Aileen.

Well that made Aileen feel a lot better even if she was annoyed by the weird emails.

Elli continued. "But I have run the phone records of Adam Jackson's old gang partner, Leo Myers. He has two phones that I know of and one of them has received a lot of calls from a burner. That could just be drug-related stuff, but I'm keeping an eye on it. As far as the Duponts, they truly do seem to be in town for the holidays. I haven't found anything odd in their browsing histories, their phone records, their financials, nothing. By all accounts, they're here visiting friends."

"I still don't like it," her mom growled. She was a petite, unassuming redhead, but she had a steel backbone and was shockingly brutal when necessary. Years ago, before she'd gone freelance, she and Aileen's dad had worked for the government. All black ops stuff. Because of her mom's unassuming appearance, she'd been used as bait more often than not—and her targets had always paid the price for underestimating her.

"I know, Mom, but I don't want you...doing anything to them." Aileen had no love for the Duponts. And after what they'd pulled, she would never let her daughter meet them, even know who they were, because she wanted separation from them. To pretend as if they didn't exist. But if her mom killed two elderly people, she couldn't handle that. She didn't want that on her conscience.

Her mom simply sniffed.

"I'm serious."

"Well we should at least attend the gala, get eyes on them," her mom insisted.

"You mean threaten them," Aileen said.

"That's not a bad idea," Elliana said before Lorna could respond.

"What?" Aileen turned on her sister-in-law.

"No, *not* threaten them, but get eyes on them. Maybe make contact, get a feel for the real reason they're in Miami, if there is another reason. I know what I've found online, but talking to them face-to-face might go a long way in giving you peace of mind," she added to Aileen's mom.

Nope. "No way is my mom going." Her mom was a lot of things, but she had no finesse. She was a sledgehammer and this situation needed diplomacy. "But I will."

Everyone looked at her with varying levels of "hell no" expressions. But too bad.

"I'm not saying I'll go alone. That would be insane. No, I mean sort of undercover. As myself, but with a date." She hadn't told Diego she wasn't going yet—because she'd been naked and distracted with Dante all last night. And a little this morning. So Diego likely still assumed she was going and she wanted to use that to her advantage. "And Elliana, I know you can get an invitation if you don't already have one."

"I...was invited," Elli grumbled. "I responded no, but it won't be a problem to change that, considering how much I already donated."

"Good, then. It's settled."

"Nothing's settled," Dante growled.

He'd been fairly quiet until now, surprising her. They'd spent the night together—but still no full-on sex because apparently he was intent on driving her crazy with need...and then Elliana had asked them to come over for a meeting.

"It's not a terrible idea," Elliana murmured.

Aileen shot her a dry look.

"No, I mean...it's good. And of course Dante will be there as backup to keep an eye on things."

"Why can't I be her date?" His tone was neutral enough as he looked at Elliana, but Aileen could feel the waves of energy rolling off him and wondered if everyone else could too.

Were they obvious or was this just her getting caught up in her thoughts?

"Because then you guys are officially linked together. If she goes with Diego, who is *not* a killer for hire, then she's just linked to some random guy she likely won't see again. If someone is watching—meaning, the Duponts—they won't find a connection between Aileen and Diego other than a superficial one. No one should be aware that you two know each other—you're perfect backup that way. And I've got a good cover you can use to attend. You can go as one of my international employees, just use a fake ID and I'll let the coordinator know I need some extra invites. This'll be easy."

Dante's jaw ticked slightly, but he eventually nodded. "Fine."

"Good, everything's settled then," Elli said, shooting Aileen's mom a hard look.

Much to Aileen's surprise. And her mom didn't say anything, another surprise. Or maybe it wasn't a surprise. For some reason her hard-ass mom seemed to have no problem letting Elli run the show. It was... Well, she wasn't sure what it was. And Aileen wasn't sure how it made her feel.

Okay, lies. She felt a *teeny* tiny bit of jealousy that her mom struggled to let Aileen out from under her wing but never questioned badass Elli. She sometimes wondered if maybe her mom wished Aileen was different, more like Elli. Hell, sometimes Aileen wished she was more like Elli.

"And you and I are having a spa day," Elli continued, looking at Aileen.

"Wait... Are you serious?" Aileen asked at the same time Dante said, "Absolutely not."

"Look, this is the most exclusive place in the city. Literally no one gets in without going through security. And it's women only. Aileen and I will be fine."

"It's secure," Theo added. "I've already fully vetted it and done some runs against their security."

"See?" Elli looked positively pleased as she squeezed her husband's leg. "This place is perfect. And Aileen...you need a manicure, pedicure and probably some other things. You deserve to be pampered. Plus we can get our hair done before the party because you know I'm not doing that shit myself."

She knew that Elli hated that kind of stuff but Aileen didn't, and getting pampered sounded wonderful. Even if she didn't want to be separated from Dante. If they were on limited time, she wanted to make the most of every minute they had together. "Okay, that's fine with me."

"I'll drive you two," Dante growled, clearly not a fan of the idea, but at least he wasn't pushing back.

Well, at least not in front of everyone, but she had a feeling he wasn't done with his objections.

CHAPTER 13

It's okay if you don't like me; not everyone has good taste.

"You know I'm just going with Diego as friends, right?" Aileen asked Elli as they got massages. She'd only agreed to go platonically to start with, so it wouldn't be a surprise to Diego. And she was ninety-nine percent sure he wasn't attracted to her anyway.

"I kind of figured," Elli murmured, her head turned toward Aileen in the dim massage room.

Soft music pumped in through hidden speakers and the scent of lavender and rosemary oil filled the air. "Why'd you figure?"

"Because of the way Dante is acting seems like an obvious thing to say but I'm saying it."

"We're just friends." With benefits. That was a thing, right?

"Sure, and I wasn't stalking my husband before we got married."

Aileen wondered what their masseuses thought of their conversation, then dismissed it because who cared. Turning away from her friend, she put her face back in the little open donut pillow as the woman working on her started pounding her calves. It shouldn't feel as good as it did, but oh my sweet Santa she could feel the stress leaving her body. "So...what if we were more than friends? I'm not saying we are, but...how do you think my parents would react?"

"Who cares?"

Aileen turned to look at her sister-in-law again. "Seriously?"

"Yep." Elli had her face in the donut now so her voice had a slightly muffled quality to it. "I love your parents. Like, love them and wish I'd had parents like them. But who cares what they think? Who cares what anyone thinks? Anyone except Nessa," she added. "Because duh. But other than her, you're the one who has to live with your choices. And you deserve to be happy."

"You make it sound so easy." She stuck her face back in the hole as a new track of soothing music came on. Elli didn't respond so Aileen did what she did best, stewed in her thoughts. She loved to dissect every little thing and make herself crazy. It was like the worst pastime ever.

When their masseuses had left and they were getting dressed again, Aileen sat on the edge of the massage table. "I'm nervous about tonight. I know what I said, but the thought of seeing...his parents, it's nerve-racking."

Nodding, Elli slid her sweater on over her head. "I know, it's why I suggested a spa day today. I figured it'd help you 'armor up.' And no one is making you go, so if you change your mind, no one will think less of you."

"I'll think less of myself," she whispered, letting the truth spill out.

Elli blinked in surprise as she crossed over to her, leaned next to her on the table. "But why?"

"I never confronted them after..." She covered her face for a long moment. "When Tanner took me to court, tried to get shared custody of Nessa, I was in a really dark place. I let my parents and Theo take over and do what they do best. Even though I'm glad he's dead now, even though I'll never, ever tell Nessa the truth about her parentage, I still feel guilty sometimes. Wondering if I should have stopped Theo, or, I don't know. Done something differently."

"Nope." Elli shook her head, so sure of herself.

"You're so confident about that," Aileen murmured, a little jealous of the other woman's constant self-assuredness.

"I guess I am. And hell, maybe I'm wrong. But that monster hurt you when you were unconscious. Took something from you that he had no right to take. Then, in an act of what I consider pure evil, tried to forcibly link you to him for the rest of your life through custody. To retraumatize you over and over. He deserved what he got and the world is a better place without him in it. If you don't want to face his parents, don't do it. But you're strong enough to do it if that's your fear. Even if they have nothing to do with what's going on right now, I think there's something to be said for facing them straight on. Maybe it'll give you closure, if you need it. But don't feel pressured to."

Aileen leaned her head on Elli's shoulder. "I'm glad you're my sister-in-law," she whispered. She always knew the right thing to say, and she'd made Theo happier than Aileen had ever seen her brother.

"Me too."

There was a soft knock at the door, their masseuses coming back to give them water and check on them. And then it was on to the last thing of the day—getting their hair done.

Aileen was nervous about tonight, about facing her past in a way she hadn't ever thought she'd be ready to. But she was also excited to see Dante's expression when he saw her after her makeover today. She knew that he liked her exactly the way she was, but screw it, she wanted him to like what he saw when he looked at her. Wanted…more than this friends-only nonsense.

But she was the one who'd put stipulations on this whole thing, had made it clear that she was asking him for a favor. Now she had to figure out how to undo that and let him know she wanted something else.

Like forever with her best friend.

CHAPTER 14

I think we become whoever would have saved
our younger selves.

Dante glanced at the tiny "sandwiches" on French baguette slices, dismissed them. He didn't want food now. He wanted to punch stuff.

"You need to do something with your face," Theo murmured as he plucked up a couple mini lobster grilled cheese appetizers from a passing server.

"What's wrong with my face?"

"You look like you're ready to commit murder. Lots and lots of murder." Theo's voice was pitched low, but it didn't matter.

Dante and he were at one of the cloth-covered high-top tables near the corner of the room with a good view of most of the exits. There was a glittery red and gold centerpiece that allowed them to use it as cover as well. Not that they needed it. They were here with invitations, in tuxes and blending nicely.

But Dante couldn't stop staring at Aileen and her date. The two of them looked good together; both slender, with the asshole tall and muscular, and they were both all shiny and polished. Though Aileen was the real star. God, she was gorgeous in that body-hugging green dress and her red hair down in big, soft-looking curls.

He just grunted at Theo, not responding one way or another. He didn't think Theo knew about him and Aileen and he certainly wasn't going to bring it up.

"I don't like how open this is," he finally said. "We don't have enough eyes on every possible threat."

"My mom's hacked into the security system and is keeping an eye out, along with Sarah in the van. My dad is also running exterior security, and you, I and Elli are all here to keep Aileen safe if necessary. And Elli pulled in some extra help—something you already know."

Dante simply grunted again. Because blah, blah, blah. Whatever. This whole night was bullshit and he hated that some asshole was here with the woman he loved.

"You sure you don't want to try these? They're really good. I might have to try making them later." Theo inhaled another one of the mini sandwiches.

"I'm fine. But her date might lose an arm. He's practically mauling her."

Theo looked at Dante, then back at his sister across the way, then pushed away from the table with an extended sigh. "I'm going to get you some food because you're clearly hangry. Dude isn't even touching her. He literally just handed her a drink and—gasp!—I think their fingers touched." Theo shook his head as he walked away.

And Dante was glad for the silence because now he could watch Aileen unimpeded. But Theo was right—he couldn't keep staring at her date as if he wanted to murder the guy. People tended to remember stuff like that.

He casually reached up to his ear and tapped the earpiece. He'd turned it off, not wanting the distraction as he scanned the place, but with Theo gone to get more food, he could listen in.

Aileen was standing with her date, Elliana, and Elliana's best friend and business partner Weston Davis. Also with Davis was his wife, musical superstar Rebel Martinez. And even though the woman was perfectly nice, she was also a magnet for everyone at the damn party, it seemed. There was a constant crowd around their little bubble, with people constantly trying to get closer to Rebel.

Luckily she had top-notch security, but there were still too many people as far as he was concerned. It was part of the reason Theo had hung back, not wanting to get caught up in any drive-by photographs.

The employees here had been strict about warning people not to take photos tonight, but people didn't always listen. Hell, their small crew had hacked the security system so he knew all he needed to know about their "security."

"I see someone we need to talk to, but we'll meet up again later," Elliana said to Weston before hugging him, then Rebel. Then she linked arms with Aileen even as her date placed his hand at the small of Aileen's back. Way too close to her bare back, considering how low the back of her dress dipped.

God, he wanted to burn the thing. Okay, lies—he loved her in it, loved how confident she'd looked earlier tonight when they'd left, and all he could think about was slowly peeling it from her body.

But he didn't like her dumb date one bit. Dante didn't care that the others had been right, that he couldn't act as her date. He didn't want her here at all.

Nope, she should be at home. *His* home, in his bed, naked. Not out here ready to confront some monsters from her past.

"Did you really see anyone?" Aileen's voice came over the comm line clearly.

Elliana snorted. "No, but it was getting too crowded for me. I forget what a mob Rebel draws."

"Are you going to her Christmas Eve party this year?" This was from Diego.

"Yeah, we'll be there," Elliana said. "How about you?"

"Maybe, we'll see." The other man was noncommittal as he glanced around, clearly paying attention to his surroundings.

Which was a point in his favor. Elliana had assured Dante that Diego knew this was a platonic thing, but Dante couldn't rein in his possessiveness where Aileen was concerned. Just couldn't seem to do it.

"Hey would you mind grabbing us drinks?" Elliana said to Diego. "I'm going to find Theo's table. He said he'd snagged one for all of us."

Diego nodded. "No problem."

As soon as the other man blended into the crowd, Elliana said, "Dante, Theo, you there?"

"Here," Dante murmured at the same time as Theo.

"Lorna's spotted one of our targets, second floor, headed toward the ladies' restroom. We're making our way there now. It's go time."

There were only two targets so this had to be Edith Dupont. Dante scanned the upper balcony but couldn't see the older woman anywhere. But he trusted Elliana and Lorna to know what they were doing. Elliana wasn't in the same line of work as them, but she'd been in the Marines and was one of the smartest people he'd ever met.

Not that he'd ever tell her that and feed her ego. *Hell no.*

Dante abandoned the table and headed around the outskirts of the crowd, making his way toward one of the sets of stairs. The party was in full swing, with a live band, an auction, and at least forty-eight Christmas trees set up around the museum's first and second floors. Or so Theo had told him. It was bright and cheery and he wished they were anywhere but here.

"What if this doesn't work?" Aileen murmured, her voice low even over the comm line.

"It'll work, you'll see." Things suddenly got quieter, then Elliana said, "We're now on the elevator."

Dante didn't have sight of them anymore as he hurried up the stairs, passing mostly couples as he tried to hurry without looking like he was.

Tension built inside him, being separated visually from Aileen. Elliana had called in outsiders to help with getting Edith Dupont alone, and on paper it was a good idea. But he knew that shit could always go sideways no matter how well planned a job was. And this was too last minute.

***

Aileen blinked in surprise as two men in tuxes approached, both carrying "wet floor" cones and one that said *under maintenance* and placed them in a half circle around the upstairs restroom door. Elli had told her that this would work, but Aileen hadn't really believed her.

A woman in all black with a little gold nametag was standing in front of the restroom and waving people away. And as soon as the women inside came out, she murmured to them, likely telling them there was an issue with the bathroom and that it was closed.

One of the men carrying a cone nodded at Elliana, pitched his voice low as he said, "You've got maybe ten minutes before anyone notices," as he set his cones down. "Get in and get out. We're leaving now."

"This is all very organized," Aileen murmured to Elli as they approached the large swinging door, the woman in black stepping back to let them through.

"I called in some favors."

"It's good luck that she decided to use this one." It was much easier to put up signs upstairs where it was less crowded.

Elli snorted. "One of the servers surreptitiously told her that the upstairs restrooms were more private and posher."

"You really called in a lot of favors."

"Eh, this one just cost a little money. People are always agreeable for cash," she whispered as she pushed the door open.

Tension and anticipation ratcheted up inside Aileen as the door swished closed quietly behind them.

The room was indeed luxurious, mostly marble with gold veining throughout the floors. There were mini gold chandeliers over the line of sinks and plush seating that made her think of long-ago parties from the roaring twenties. The seafoam-colored round, tufted ottoman in the center of the room had dividers to give people privacy if needed.

Two women were washing their hands as Elli quickly went from stall to stall, looking for Edith Dupont.

Luckily the other women weren't paying attention to them at all before they dried their hands and headed out, whispering to each other about someone's shoes.

Elli motioned with her hand that this was it when the toilet flushed.

In that moment Aileen questioned this entire thing. Maybe she was making a huge mistake. Maybe the Duponts were simply in town to see friends and their appearance had nothing to do with... The bathroom door opened and Edith

Dupont stepped out.

She had on a sparkly pale pink gown, and even though she was in her seventies, her hair was still an almost platinum blonde in a perfect bob that probably cost a lot to upkeep.

Aileen's first instinct was to turn around or hide, but screw it. Someone had targeted her. Twice. Dressed like Santa, which somehow made it all the worse. And she wasn't that scared college student anymore who'd been sheltered her entire life.

Elli simply nodded at her as she sat on the velvet ottoman and crossed her legs.

This was it, the only chance she might ever get. "Mrs. Dupont."

The woman turned as she walked toward the sinks, her expression expectant, but the moment her gaze landed on Aileen, she froze, her blue eyes wide.

Blue eyes the same color as her rapist.

Aileen was just grateful that Nessa took after her.

The older woman blinked, cleared her throat, then blinked again, and her face had gone ghostly pale. "What are you doing here?" she finally rasped out.

"I'm here to see you." Aileen took a step toward her, her heels clicking softly on the floor. She was glad her voice didn't shake.

The woman held up her hands almost defensively and shot Elli a beseeching look.

Elli simply buffed her nails on her dress as she looked bored.

It took Mrs. Dupont exactly two seconds to realize that Elli was with her. "We've done everything your parents asked," the woman rasped out, her voice trembling. And in that moment, she looked frail, old. She sagged against the nearby sink, clutched onto it with her perfectly manicured hands. "We've never reached out, never even looked you up. So why are you here?"

"Because someone mugged me, then another person tried to carjack me, and both of them were dressed like Santa. And it's all happening while you and your husband are in town. It doesn't feel like a coincidence."

The woman's fear bled away to be replaced by confusion. "I have no idea about any Santas or whatever you're talking about. Friends asked us here last minute and a Miami Christmas sounded better than a Vermont one."

"I suggest this is the last Christmas you visit." Elli stood now, her voice shards of ice.

Aileen looked at her sister-in-law in surprise. She'd never heard the other woman sound so cold. So...deadly.

"Are you sure your husband didn't...hire someone?" Aileen asked, wanting to cover all her bases. Because she actually believed the woman. Her fear was real at least, and her surprise seemed authentic as well.

Edith Dupont made a slight scoffing sound. "He didn't do anything either. He's barely recovered from the loss of... From our loss." She turned to the sink then, started washing her hands as she continued. "We're just trying to live quiet lives."

Aileen didn't respond, simply nodded as the woman dried her hands.

"Am I free to go or are you going to hurt me? Threaten me?" Mrs. Dupont asked.

"No one is hurting anyone. We're just two women having a conversation." Aileen was proud that her voice still didn't tremble when inside she felt as if she was coming apart at the seams.

The older woman straightened, looking more like the person Aileen knew from pictures. A proud, wealthy woman who came from old, old money. "We'll be leaving the day after Christmas," she finally said as she started for the exit, her low heels clicking. Then she turned. "How is...your daughter?"

"Perfect."

Lips tight, she nodded but didn't stride off as Aileen had expected. Instead, she continued, "For the record, I didn't raise him to be..." She cleared her throat, seemed to struggle to find any words at all, then simply said, "I'm sorry."

As soon as she was gone, Aileen nearly collapsed and found herself being pulled into a big hug by Elli, which was the bigger surprise.

Elli didn't say anything, just wrapped her up in a tight embrace before she pulled back. "I hate to say this, but I believe her."

"I do too," Aileen muttered. Which meant they were still at square one.

When the door opened again, they stepped apart and headed out past a woman with an official-looking nametag on. She had on a long, black dress and was looking around in confusion and maybe a bit of concern.

"I'm sorry to bother you," the woman said, "but I was told that there were maintenance signs up here? That someone was telling people to use different restrooms?"

Elli shook her head, her expression guileless. "We haven't seen anything like that. But I must say what a lovely evening this has been. You've really outdone yourself with the food and the auction this year. It's even better than last year."

Aileen murmured and nodded her agreement with Elli, not surprised when the woman beamed at her.

"Well thank you, we've put quite a lot of work into and we're grateful for all you've given as well," she said as the three of them strode from the room. There were two security guys subtly standing off to the side, but the woman quickly waved them off and said, "It was a miscommunication," as she continued chatting to Elli all the way downstairs.

As they reached the bottom of the stairs, Aileen could see Diego at one of the high-top tables waiting for them—and Dante standing near a pillar, a full champagne glass in hand.

He looked good enough to eat, and whew, the way he was looking at her was almost enough to make her combust. She wondered how long she had to stay here now. Could they all just leave? And then could she head back to Dante's place for the rest of the night?

As she made her way to the table with Elli, she smiled at a familiar face. "Calvin," she said, pausing by a table with one of the dads from the soccer field. His daughter played with another team, but at this age all the kids played at the same set of fields.

He blinked once, looking almost confused as he swept a gaze over her. "Ah…"

"Nessa's mom, from soccer," she supplied, laughing lightly.

He smiled, but it looked almost forced. "Right, right. Ah, Aileen right?"

She nodded and smiled at the pretty, dark-haired woman next to him. And got a frosty, tight-lipped smile in return. *Okay, then.*

"Well, have a great evening," she murmured and continued with Elli, who simply raised her eyebrows.

"The tension from those two...yikes," Elli murmured as they reached the table with Theo and Diego.

Right? Even as the others started making small talk, her gaze strayed to where Dante had been standing.

But he wasn't there. Disappointment punctured through her, but she forced herself to smile as she turned back to the others.

She'd just faced down her past. She could deal with a stupid party for a little longer.

CHAPTER 15

Dear Santa, define naughty.

As the valet pulled up with Theo's SUV, Aileen nearly jolted when Dante slid up next to them, whisper quiet. Or maybe assassin quiet was more accurate.

Diego had already left (thankfully, and yes, she felt bad even thinking that) and she was glad to have it just be the people she cared about now. Even if they were back to square one with the whole mugger thing, or *still* at square one—whatever, she was simply happy to be with Dante again.

Though she schooled her expression, hoping her brother didn't notice the way she was looking at Dante. Elli seemed to know about her and Dante, or at least guess, but she didn't think Theo did. Because she was pretty sure he'd have said something to her.

"You look really nice tonight," she whispered, skating her fingers against Dante's as Theo slid into the driver's seat.

"You look gorgeous and I plan to make you come against my face later tonight," Dante growled before he opened the back door for her.

Heat punched through her at his words as she slid into the back seat. What was he trying to do to her?

"I might have found something," Dante said once they'd shut all the doors and Theo had pulled away from the curb. "On your ASMR videos."

"What did you find?" Elli asked from the front passenger seat even as Aileen frowned, clearly wondering what he could have discovered that she hadn't. Because Elliana was thorough.

"On the twelfth, during one of your whisper videos, you mention going on a date." He said the word *date* with barely concealed distaste. "It's all part of the dialogue and near the end. Then in this video you talk about how people can give to certain toy drop-offs in the Miami area and what you're doing to help. You specifically mention the one you're going to be volunteering at."

"So?" Aileen knew about that because she'd *made* the videos. In them she tapped on various surfaces while she whispered random things about her day or week or things that interested her in general. Sometimes she rambled about books or music and other times she whispered about random life thoughts.

It was just supposed to be calming for people who needed to relax or sleep. And she was pretty sure most people didn't even actually hear what she was saying. When she listened to whisper videos to sleep, she simply liked the consistent lulling sound, not the content.

"You're basically telling people where you're going in whispers. What if whoever is targeting you used that to pinpoint your location? Because so far no one has come to your house, to the neighborhood. The Santas have tried to attack you in public. And we know that the first Santa at least was hired, and I'm guessing the second was too."

"Maybe, but I don't see how they'd have figured out it was me from the videos."

"You might hide most of your face, but your hair is distinctive. And in this video," he held out the first one, "you're wearing the same sweater as you were the day the second Santa tried to carjack you. I haven't looked back farther, but I'm guessing that there are plenty of videos where you share personal things without meaning to. Someone could have used that to build a picture of the places you'd be."

"Damn it," Elli muttered from the front. "I was looking for trolls and weirdos, threatening messages, not something like this in my scans. My programs wouldn't have picked this up anyway."

Ice slid through Aileen as she thought about all the random "conversations" she'd had on her videos. Because of her family's profession, she'd always been careful of her privacy and she'd never mentioned Nessa in any of them. Nothing to do with soccer practices or anything like that. It was all very benign but...maybe not as benign as she'd thought. Sometimes it was stream of consciousness type of ramblings.

"Maybe someone found me that way, and this is a big maybe," Aileen said. "But what's the purpose? Seriously, why? *Why* would someone want my phone? That's the real question." And one they'd gone over so many times—with no answer.

***

"You're supposed to be asleep," Aileen murmured as she slid on top of the covers next to Nessa, who was fighting to stay awake. She was sleeping at Aileen's parents tonight.

"I know," she said around a yawn. "I wanted to see you in your fancy dress. You look really pretty, mommy."

Oooh, the mommy got her every time. More and more Nessa simply called her "mom" but sometimes her girl slipped a "mommy" in there and Aileen soaked it in. This time with her was so precious, so limited, and she wanted to savor all of it even as it felt like time was slipping through her fingers.

"Thank you."

"How was the party? Did your date look handsome? Did Dante look handsome?"

She paused at the Dante question. "Dante looked very handsome and my date did too. But my date and I are just friends. I don't think we'll be going on any more dates."

"Oh, good," she murmured, her eyes drifting closed again as she clearly lost the battle with sleep. "Otherwise Santa's answering to me..."

Aileen frowned as she brushed back a few strands of Nessa's wayward curls. "Nessa?"

Her daughter didn't respond though, just curled on her side and clutched her favorite pillow, a stuffed pink and neon yellow soccer ball.

When Aileen stepped out into the hallway, her dad was waiting for her, a soft smile on his face. "She really wanted to see you in that dress," he murmured, kissing the top of her head. "And she was convinced that you and your mom were at a party having fun without her."

"If only. I'm now more frustrated than before."

"Really?" he asked as they descended the stairs.

"Maybe... No. I'm frustrated about the whole situation but at least we were able to eliminate two suspects." Or she was pretty sure they had. "Edith Dupont was almost scared to see me," she said as they reached the bottom stair, stepped into the foyer. Aileen wondered if that made her small for being glad—she'd rather the woman be afraid of her than see her as a target. Because fear meant the woman would keep her distance from Nessa.

"Good." Her quiet father, always short on words, didn't disappoint now with his response.

Sighing, she simply hugged him tight. "I love you, Dad. And thank you for watching Nessa tonight. I'll see you in the morning."

He nodded and walked outside with her, watching her head home. She wondered if her dad knew about her and Dante, but then dismissed that almost immediately. He'd definitely have something to say about that if he had any suspicion. Her mom certainly would too, which was why Aileen was making her escape before her mother returned from Elli and Theo's place.

She waved at her dad as she stepped past her front door, then shut and locked it—right as strong arms wrapped around her from behind.

CHAPTER 16

Keep calm and get your ho, ho, ho on.

Aileen leaned back into Dante's hold, glad he was waiting for her. "So what did you guys find?" she murmured as he nuzzled her neck. Shivers rolled through her as he nipped at her earlobe.

He and the others had been at Theo and Elli's place going over the videos in more depth even though it was already late. But the three of them, and her mom, hadn't been ready to call it a night so she'd left them to kiss Nessa good night.

"I don't want to talk about them," he growled. "I just want to get that dress off you."

She knew she should probably care more about what the others were doing, considering it was her safety at risk, but she couldn't dredge up much when Dante was sliding his big hands down over her waist—and tugging her dress up to her hips.

"I hated seeing you on a date tonight."

"Wasn't a date," she rasped out.

"Well I don't want you dating anyone." His words were a rumbly growl against her neck that sent shivers down her spine.

"What about you?" she asked, forcing the words out. They'd never talked about him or if he dated or...what he did when he was off on jobs.

He paused before turning her around, caging her against the front door. As he looked down at her with undisguised heat in his dark eyes, he frowned. "What about me?"

"Are you...dating anyone?" She didn't think he was, but she wanted it spelled out. Clearly.

He slid his palm between her legs, cupped her mound—and found out that she wasn't wearing anything under her dress. He groaned as he leaned down, nipped her bottom lip. "Not dating anyone," he murmured against her mouth.

"So, what is this thing between us, then?" How she was even managing to get words out when he slipped a finger inside her was a mystery. She clenched around him, wanting a lot more than this. Tonight she wanted everything.

"What do you want it to be?" Now he kissed along her jawline as he added another finger.

She clutched onto his shoulders, digging in as she tried to steady herself. "That's not an answer."

He gently raked his teeth over her bare shoulder, sending another shiver spiraling through her. "Already told you I'm not sharing."

"Neither will I." Now she dug in with her fingernails.

He pulled back slightly, pinning her with his dark gaze as much as he was with his hands and body. "I haven't been with anyone since I met you." His words were low, growly and...

Wait, what?

He couldn't be serious. That had been *years* ago. She clenched around both his fingers as he stroked inside her, slowly, wonderfully and, oh god, he felt so damn good. "Are you serious?" she managed to rasp out.

"Very serious." He claimed her mouth, stealing her breath and her words as he practically devoured her.

She had questions, but then he unzipped the back of her dress, and yep, screw talking. He made her feel safe in a way she never thought she would again. She wanted to revisit the whole "haven't been with anyone since I met you" thing but... *Oh!* He nipped her earlobe, then raked his teeth over her neck aaaand he was making his way lower, lower... He sucked one nipple into his mouth and she arched against him.

Her dress had fallen to her waist, but he hadn't unzipped it fully so it was bunched up at her hips, baring her to him in all the right places.

After teasing both her nipples into tight points, he, oooh, he was kneeling in front of her. And she realized he was doing exactly what he'd said earlier.

"Spread your legs a little," he growled.

"We're doing this right here?" Did her voice squeak a little? Yep. She'd just been picturing this differently, like in a bed. But he seemed obsessed with going down on her.

"Are you good with this?" When he looked up at her with those dark eyes and a face that would make angels weep, she nodded. But he wasn't having it. "I need to hear it."

Somehow she found her voice. "More than good."

The look he gave her was so hungry, so all-consuming, she felt it all the way to her core.

And when he slid one of her ankles over his shoulder, she couldn't think of anything else as he teased and pleasured her until he pulled a sharp, toe-curling orgasm from her with his mouth and fingers. Before she'd come down from her climax, he moved fast, scooping her up in his arms and carrying her up to her room.

To a bed she'd never shared with anyone else and nothing about that mattered right now. Because she wanted something real with Dante, not just for him to help her get over fears. She wanted a future with him.

"Dante…" She cleared her throat, tried to find her voice, but it was hard when he was stripping off his tuxedo jacket, then his shirt.

Each button he slid out, all she could do was stare hungrily. It was like watching the best strip show ever because it was all for her. And it was Dante.

"I love it when you watch me like that." His voice shook slightly as he discarded his shirt. When his fingers skimmed the top of his pants, he stilled, his dark gaze on her, a question in his eyes.

"Take them off." Did she sound like she was begging? Well, it wasn't far from the truth.

"Only if you take off yours." He was doing that growly, sexy thing that sent shivers spiraling throughout her.

She still had her dress halfway on, and while she'd been bared to him before, this felt different. Tonight felt different, maybe because they were on the same page. Or she really hoped they were. She'd spent so many years afraid of being vulnerable again, of getting hurt again, but she couldn't hide from everything.

And she didn't want to hide from Dante anyway. Never.

As he slid his pants off, she finished shimmying out of her dress, and she soaked in the groan he let out as he reached for her.

"Can't believe you weren't wearing anything under your dress." He sounded almost pained, and oh wow, she could only stare at the thick outline under his boxer briefs. And when he slid them off, she sucked in a breath.

She'd seen him before, touched him before, but apparently it would take some time getting used to the sight of him.

They moved toward each other at the same time and thankfully he was taking over, because she might be ready for this, but she was still in unchartered territory.

As they kissed, he walked them to the bed, and to her surprise he stretched out underneath her so that she had to straddle him.

He clasped onto her hips as she settled on top of him. "You set the pace. Anytime you want to stop, just tell me and we stop. You're in control."

Her inner walls tightened at his words, at this man who was doing everything to make this good for her. Thankfully they'd already talked about birth control and they were both clean (though he hadn't mentioned not being with anyone for years!). Since she was on birth control, no worries there either.

She leaned forward slightly so that her folds rubbed against his thick erection, and the look on his face, the groan he made... She could come from that alone.

His fingers flexed against her hip as he reached up with his other hand, cupped the back of her head and kissed her like he'd been starving for her.

She found herself swept away in his kiss, swept away in everything that he was, and shed the lingering fears she'd been holding on to as she lost herself with him.

Heat pooled between her legs as he cupped one of her breasts, lazily strummed one of her nipples until she was groaning from the pleasure of it.

Each time he teased her nipple or grazed his thumb over her pulsing clit, she knew it wasn't going to take long for her to come once he was inside her because she was absolutely primed for him. And she really wanted to come with him inside her, especially this first time between them. Going on instinct, she leaned forward so that his thick head was right at her entrance, teasing.

"You're sure?" he growled against her mouth.

In response, she slid down on him, her head falling back as she adjusted to his size. *Ooh, wow.* She sucked in a breath as she settled on him, savored the feel of his fullness as he stretched her. Over the years she'd played with toys but this was so much different.

Better.

"Feel...amazing," she managed to rasp out.

He gritted his teeth as he struggled to remain still underneath her. Or he looked like he was struggling with his jaw clenched.

Keeping her gaze on him, she slowly rolled her hips, watching his reaction even as he filled her, hit her in spots she'd only fantasized about.

He made a low growling sound as she rolled her hips over him again.

He clutched his fingers on her hips, stilled her. "You're perfection, but I need a second." He gritted out the words as if they were a confession.

And something about the strain in his voice, the way his throat was cording tight... She rolled her hips again, grinned wickedly when he let out another groan.

"I want to feel you coming inside me," she whispered as she started moving her hips in a slow, steady rhythm. There was so much she wanted to try with him, but he'd been right about her being on top this first time.

She liked being in control, loved watching his facial expressions flitter between hunger and, well, desperation.

He rolled his own hips up to meet her, hitting her even deeper, and she could feel another orgasm starting to build—probably because she was already so worked up for him.

And also, his dick was amazing.

Something she needed to tell him, but no words would come as he pulled back, thrust again. Completely letting go of her control, she met him stroke for stroke, riding him as he held on to her hips possessively.

She had a feeling he would leave marks and was glad for it.

"I'm so close. I need...just a little more." And she was too nervous to touch herself. She figured that one day she'd be comfortable, but not today.

Thankfully he reached between their bodies and began teasing her clit without any more prompting. Aaand, oh, she was definitely going to come.

The sensation of him filling her, his thick length stroking that magic spot deep inside combined with this and... Her inner walls clenched around him faster and harder as her climax crested higher and higher.

"Dante!" She cried out his name as it hit, pleasuring spilling out to all her nerve endings as she came.

Just like that, she saw him let go of his own control, as if something had physically snapped inside him. He thrust upward on a cry, coming inside her in long, hard strokes.

She wasn't sure how long they lost themselves inside each other, but eventually she collapsed on him and could have lay there all night. But he gently nudged her off him as he murmured, "Be right back."

Feeling way too good, she stretched out on the bed and stared up at the ceiling, wondering how long they'd have to wait to do that again. Because she was greedy and wanted so much more.

He was back moments later with a washcloth in hand. When he knelt next to her and began wiping between her legs, she wanted to cry and kiss him at the same time. "You're always so thoughtful," she murmured, stroking her fingers down his forearm, loving that she got to touch him the way she wanted now.

No more just fantasizing.

He snorted softly before he tossed the cloth down and stretched out next to her. "You're pretty much the only person to ever say that." He kissed the top of her head as he pulled her close. "How are you feeling?"

"Amazing. God, you felt so good. I didn't realize...you're incredible."

His grip around her tightened as she half splayed over his chest. "You're good for my ego. And you're the incredible one. Better than I fantasized about."

Surprised, she lifted her head. "You fantasized about me?"

Even more surprising, his cheeks flushed with just a tinge of pink. "Probably more than I should admit," he finally said.

She laughed lightly. "Glad I'm not the only one." Idly, she traced over a scar on his left pec, long faded and a pale white half-moon against his tanned skin. "What's this from?"

He covered her hand with his, then brought her fingers up to his mouth, kissed each one. When he didn't answer, she thought maybe she'd hit on a sore subject.

"You don't have to tell me."

"No, I want to. It's just...this particular scar was from my uncle."

They'd been friends for years so she knew that his uncle had raised him after his mom died of emergency surgery complications. His father had disappeared when he was born and it had been him and his mom until he was twelve. "Intentional-ly?"

His jaw ticked once. "Yeah."

She blinked, then frowned as she looked at it again—then noticed a few more scattered over his carved abs. Some of them blended with the curves of his mus-cles. "Did he...cut you?"

"Burned me. It's not as bad as it could have been," he rushed out when she let out a little gasp. "Once I got big enough, I fought back and that was that. He never touched me again."

Horrified for him, she wrapped her arms around him, wishing someone had been there to protect him. "I'm sorry, I didn't realize."

He lifted a shoulder even as he tightened his hold on her. "I don't talk about it. It's in the past and he's dead—not from me. Cirrhosis of the liver."

"Well I'm still sorry."

"I had a lot of good years with my mom." He said it so matter-of-fact, but she knew that kind of loss would cut deep. Then he added, "Not enough, but they were good and I hold on to those memories."

She wasn't sure what it said about her, but she was glad his uncle was dead. And she hated that he'd experienced that kind of loss so young.

She kissed his bare chest before settling against him, savoring the quiet of it just being the two of them. But her curious nature eventually won out. "Can I ask you something?"

"Anything." His voice was a deep, comforting rumble.

"Did you really mean what you said...about not being with anyone since meeting me?"

"Yep." He lazily stroked his hand down her spine, cupped one butt cheek, squeezed. "I met you and that was it, Aileen."

Oh. Ooooh. That wasn't what she'd been expecting. Unsure how to respond, she kissed his chest, then continued kissing lower and lower until she realized he was ready to go again.

Smiling against the tip of his erection, she looked up at him, saw him watching her with a wild hunger right before he took over.

Moving faster than should have been possible, he had her flat on her back and his face between her legs again. And when he went down on her, it was with a hunger that matched her own. One that told her he was definitely as obsessed as she was.

CHAPTER 17

I don't always put my foot in my mouth, but when I do, I put both feet in.

"Hey, Nessa's working on something for Christmas with my mom so I've got some time," Aileen said as she sat down with her laptop in Theo and Elli's living room. "And I've gone over notes I kept from various videos over the last six months to try to streamline which videos we're looking closer at. Because no one's messed with me since recently so...this has to be a new thing."

Sitting next to her, Elliana nodded as she turned her own laptop toward Aileen, kicked her feet up on the ottoman. "The videos are important but the why of your cell phone is the root." She shook her head slightly. "And I still can't find anything on any of your videos. I did find a comment you made once about recording your ASMR videos on your phone so maybe there is a link. I just...don't know what." And her sister-in-law sounded absolutely ready to pull her hair out.

Theo was sitting on a smaller chair, catty-corner of them, his gaze on the muted television above the electric fireplace. It wasn't cold enough to turn it on but they had the flames going, giving the room a nice glow.

Aileen's gaze flickered to the TV and she saw the face of a teacher who'd been missing for the last few weeks on-screen. "They found her?" she murmured.

Her brother nodded and turned up the TV. As he did, she heard the front door open then close and when she glanced over her shoulder, she saw Dante striding in. They hadn't wanted to arrive at the same time because she needed to tell her family about the two of them. First, however, she wanted to tell Nessa. When she met his gaze, her cheeks heated at the dark look he gave her. She murmured a greeting before turning back to the TV.

The solemn-faced newscaster was still talking. "The body of beloved teacher Christina Fraser has been found in the Everglades by a tour boat. It appears to be a fluke that she was found at all and it's clear that whoever committed this horrible crime wanted to…"

Dante sat on the edge of the couch close to her, made a disappointed sound. "I figured this was how it would end."

Yeah, Aileen had too, but she'd been holding on to a little hope for the beautiful teacher who'd been missing since the beginning of the month. Her face had been splashed everywhere when she hadn't shown up to work. And not just in Florida, her face had been shown nationwide. Probably because she was a platinum blonde with extraordinary good looks. And she'd once done some modeling before she found her passion of teaching. And Aileen knew it had to be a passion because the pay was crap.

"Poor woman," Aileen murmured. Hadn't shown up to work and had been seen leaving her condo the night before she'd disappeared around eight o'clock. There had been no footage of her returning so the police had a good idea of when she'd been taken. Unfortunately it didn't seem they knew much more. Or they weren't sharing it with the public.

"Do they know who did it?" Elli asked without looking up from her own laptop.

Sighing, Theo muted the TV as he said, "Doesn't seem that way."

"Can you turn it off, Theo?" Aileen murmured, not wanting to watch it as they went over stuff. It was too depressing. Her brother nodded as he lifted the remote control. "Since last night was a bust, I wanted to ask you guys what you thought about me dropping another video tonight? One I would create with the sole intention of leaving clues about some place I'll be tomorrow. Nothing too obvious, but enough to bait a Santa into coming after me."

"Hell. No," Dante growled before she'd finished.

"It's not a terrible idea." Elli still didn't look up from her laptop as she scanned another video.

Not terrible? Aileen would take it. "Yeah, and I'm not saying I'll go off on my own. If you would let me *finish*, I was thinking that we could set up whoever is behind this. Like a little sting or whatever. At least bring them out into public, or someone they hired. We have absolutely no leads and I don't want to keep living in fear." And more importantly, she wanted to keep her daughter safe. "So we could take control of the situation, drop some hints that I'll be somewhere of our choosing. This way it changes the dynamics."

"No way." Dante was already shaking his head.

"It's...not bad." Theo cleared his throat when Dante shot him a dark look. "If we're baiting whoever this is, or someone they hire, we're in charge. Aileen won't be blindsided or in danger because we'll all be there. We'll recruit some others too so it's not a small group."

"We could ask Sarah. She's been bored," Aileen said. The former hitman had retired at the top of her game, and had been trying to do all sorts of things to fill her time since then. Sarah loved crocheting, but said she needed something more. She needed a project and this could be perfect. "And Hudson doesn't have any jobs lined up until after the New Year. We could ask him too."

Dante's dark gaze swiveled to hers. "How do you know Hudson doesn't have any jobs?"

She blinked. "Uh, because he told me."

"You're not doing this."

She blinked again, staring at him in shock. "Um, excuse me?"

"You're not doing this. You're not putting yourself in danger."

Elli cleared her throat. "If it's a controlled environment—"

"No." Dante's tone was resolute.

"You're not in charge of me." Aileen slid her laptop onto the ottoman and faced Dante.

"Well someone needs to be."

She was aware of Elli sucking in a breath and couldn't see her brother's face, but she didn't care about them. She couldn't believe the way Dante was acting right now. "Someone needs to be in charge of me? Someone other than me?" Oh, she was definitely raising her voice now.

"I...didn't mean it like that."

"Sure sounds like it."

"I'm just saying that this is dangerous and stupid."

"Oh, so now my idea is stupid? Am I stupid?" Okay, she was pushing his buttons now and knew it, but he'd pissed her off. Insinuating that she needed someone to take care of her... It was her hot button.

"That's not what I said at all!" He stood now and paced to the fireplace, looked at Theo beseechingly.

Her brother, to her surprise, didn't say a damn word, simply looked back and forth between the two of them, his eyes a little wide. *Good.* This wasn't his business.

She kept her gaze pinned on Dante. "I'm not talking about running into a situation half-cocked. I've thought this out thoroughly and would have the best backup—and I wouldn't be alone. We'd choose a public place, and we have so many people in the neighborhood and beyond who would happily help with this. It makes more sense to do this now and make this person come to us instead of waiting for something bad to happen later."

"No, this isn't happening."

Okay, that was it. Standing, she snagged her laptop up and tucked it under her arm. "I'm done with this. Just because we're sleeping together doesn't mean you can tell me what to do. Order me around as if...well, whatever. You don't get to tell me what to do as if you know better than me."

She probably shouldn't have said the whole "sleeping together" thing in front of her brother, but she was an adult. Her family could deal with it because she was absolutely over everyone treating her as if she didn't know her own mind.

Aileen turned to look at Elli. "I'll leave it up to you and Theo to come up with a place I can mention in tonight's video. I've already got a handful of videos completed, so if anything, I can add in some whispering and just splice it in to make it flow. I'm heading over to my parents to spend time with Nessa and them... Just call or text once you've figured things out." Because it was a great plan, she felt it to her bones. Having a controlled environment was the best option in a lot of shitty ones that involved her waiting around in fear.

"Aileen—"

"Dante, I don't want to do this right now. I need some space." She left without waiting for his response because she couldn't deal with his high-handedness right now.

Or ever.

This was a side of Dante she'd never seen and couldn't deal with. She'd never thought in terms of deal-breakers, but this... This type of attitude was one.

She was just starting to spread her wings again and she wouldn't let anyone clip them. And he'd just shut down her idea without listening to it fully. Just decided that he knew best.

She couldn't be with someone who wouldn't listen to her.

CHAPTER 18

Dear Santa, I regret nothing.

"So...have you talked to Dante since yesterday?" Elli didn't look over from the driver's seat as she pulled into the parking lot of the year-round Christmas store they'd chosen for their sting operation.

Aileen shook her head. "Nope."

This place was popular, but it wasn't connected to other stores and didn't have many exits. They'd recruited half a dozen hitmen from the neighborhood to help out with recon and security. Aileen wasn't sure who'd come up with this as the final place, but it was the one Elli and Theo had told her to include in the video she'd dropped last night.

One way or another, they'd find out if her stalker or whoever was watching. She'd mentioned this place eight times in her whispers and made it clear she'd be here.

"I'm not trying to defend him or anything, but men can be dumb sometimes when they're in love."

She glanced over at Elli in horror. "He doesn't...love me!" She stuttered over the last two words. "That's not what this is about. He's being controlling and acting totally out of character."

"Well, maybe." Elli's tone was annoyingly calm.

"What do you mean, *maybe*? You heard him."

"Eh, yeah, but Theo kidnapped me when he was worried about keeping me safe."

"And you tried to choke him out because of it so don't pretend like you weren't pissed." She'd only found out those details much later—Aileen hadn't even known about the kidnapping when it happened. And she wanted to say she couldn't believe her brother had kidnapped Elliana, but those two were into some weird stuff so...she wasn't exactly surprised.

"True. But I still banged him and things worked out."

"I don't even know what to say to that," she murmured, glancing out the tinted window of Elli's vehicle.

"You don't have to say anything. I know you've got a lot to deal with, but Dante isn't your enemy. He just wants to keep you safe and he has a stupid way of showing it. I just don't want you to forget that when emotions are high."

"I can't believe you of all people are standing up for him."

"Why me of all people?" Elli sounded indignant.

She glanced at the blonde bombshell, eyebrows raised. "You act like you hate him sometimes. You two literally compete over giving Nessa gifts." And the trash talk between the two of them was wild.

"I don't understand why people are saying that. I like Dante... I just really, really like to win stuff too. And being number one for Nessa's affection is an honorable goal."

Despite the turmoil churning inside her, Aileen snort-laughed. "You're such a weirdo."

"I know." Elli grinned, then handed over a little earpiece. "Your earpiece is muted on your end, but everyone else will be able to hear you. That way you don't get distracted by people talking. You want to go over everything before we head inside?"

"No... Maybe. Fine, yes. Okay, so you and I head in together, then after a few minutes we go our separate ways to 'shop' and then I take my time in the outdoor section since it's pretty open. And Hudson and Sarah will be on the exits out there so no one can kidnap me or whatever."

"Yes. Also, Dante will be moving around independently from everyone else. He won't be making eye contact or anything, but he'll be there in the background, keeping you safe, along with the others. We're all going to be close."

Aileen didn't say anything one way or another, but she was grateful he was there even if she was annoyed with him. He'd texted her last night wanting to talk, but she hadn't been ready. Maybe...maaaaybe she understood him being overprotective. But they couldn't start a relationship on unequal footing. That way lay madness. "Okay, let's do this," she said as she slipped the earpiece in. "Testing."

"I hear you," Elli said, giving her a thumbs-up.

"And I can't hear anything on my end."

"Good, it's working. Let's go."

Once they were inside the Christmas wonderland (which felt more like Christmas on cocaine) she and Elli "shopped" before Elli went to look at stocking stuffers and Aileen headed toward the outdoor displays of realistic-looking Christmas trees. Despite it being so close to Christmas, people were milling about, buying all sizes of trees.

After two hours of no weird interaction and no Santa sightings other than the solo Santa who worked at the shop, she was starting to wonder if they'd made a mistake.

Then a scream rent the air.

As panic punched through her, she turned, ready to defend herself or someone else, but found a four-year-old screaming at the top of her lungs as she raced past Aileen that she wasn't taking a picture with "a bearded weirdo stranger!", her mother in tow behind her.

Aileen snort-laughed to herself as she came up to a giant rack of ornaments. When she spotted a couple soccer-themed ones, she snagged them, figuring she could add them to the little tree in Nessa's room.

"Hey, Nessa's mom." A semi-familiar sounding voice made her turn.

She blinked, gave a cautious smile to Calvin True, the soccer dad she'd seen at the gala the other night. "Hey."

He was a lot more casual now than he'd been the other night, his smile welcoming. "Fancy running into you again. Last-minute shopping?"

Smiling, she held up one of the sparkly soccer ornaments. "She doesn't need anything else but I can't help myself. What about you?'

"Yeah, my wife and I are grabbing a couple last-minute things for her parents who decided to visit a couple days ago." His expression was dry, but charming. "Look, I'm sorry about the other night. I know your name is Aileen, it was just seeing you out of context that threw me off, if that makes sense."

"Oh, I don't care if you don't remember my name, it's fine." She waved it off. She couldn't remember all of the parents from the soccer teams either.

He rubbed the back of his neck, almost absently. "I know, but my... I feel like maybe my wife was a little rude and I'm sorry. We were dealing with some stuff and you happened to walk by at that time."

She nodded slightly. "I get it. The holidays are tough sometimes. We pile too much on ourselves."

"Yes," he said on a laugh. "I'm ready for Christmas to be over." Wincing, he looked around as he said it. "Probably shouldn't admit that in here. I'll end up with coal in my stocking."

She snickered at his dumb joke, then nodded politely as he continued on past her, grabbing one of the soccer ornaments for himself.

Briefly she wondered if he could be behind the Santa muggings, but no, seeing him at the gala had been a fluke and not the first of its kind. She hadn't mentioned it in any of her videos either so that was out.

Wondering if she should start looking for Elli, she jolted when Calvin's wife stepped in front of her little cart. "I know who you are, whore. Stay away from my husband!" the pretty brunette hissed, her tone low.

Startled, she took a step back even as she was glad for the barrier of the cart. "I have no idea what you're talking about." She glanced around the various display racks, but there wasn't anyone close enough to overhear them. Though she spotted one of her neighbors who was part of this sting and he simply nodded so she knew he was keeping an eye out.

Thankfully the woman didn't take another step forward. She just raised a huge garlic and herb cheese log, according to the packaging, and shook it slightly at Aileen. "Lie all you want, I know the truth. If you know what's good for you, you'll end things. If not..." The dark look she sliced at Aileen sent a chill down her spine.

Before she could think of a response—other than running from the wild-eyed woman—the brunette turned and stomped away, clutching her cheese.

Elli was suddenly there, then she saw Dante and Theo behind a rack of ugly Christmas sweaters and she could breathe again.

Elli slid up next to her and linked her arm with hers. "We're going to check out and act like everything is normal, but Sarah is going to tail that woman just in case."

"That was so weird," she murmured, more to herself than Elli. And incredibly stressful.

"Yeah, that woman isn't playing with a full deck." Elli kept her expression neutral as she basically guided Aileen to the checkout. "And we've got some weird Santa movement out in the parking lot. A guy dressed as Santa is sitting in a beater near the front of the store just watching people come and go. It's creepy o'clock."

"You think it's a mugger?"

"I don't know, but we're going to see if he follows you. If he does, he won't get close to you. Don't worry."

Aileen nodded as they got in line, resisting the urge to turn around and look for Dante. She needed to act normal in case anyone was watching. After she'd paid for her few things and they headed for the exit doors, Elli murmured, "Leave your purse in the cart."

"What?"

"Your mom is going to grab yours and leave a fake. This is all on the fly but Dante thinks that if you pop the trunk and leave your purse in the cart, it'll give any would-be mugger a perfect opportunity to snag it and run. And then we can follow him that way."

Oh, that was really smart. Aileen set her black purse in the cart next to her red and white shopping bags, and as they walked out the doors, her mom smoothly picked up Aileen's purse and replaced it with a dark brown one.

"God, she's good." There was awe in Elli's voice as they kept going, Aileen pushing the cart behind a big cluster of senior citizens wearing sparkly red fanny packs.

"Right?" One of her mom's greatest skills was getting into places unseen and unheard. And lifting things right under people's noses. She'd taught Aileen some of it growing up, but Aileen would never be as smooth as Lorna, a woman who'd grown up on the streets.

"Oh, I see him," Aileen said as she slid her sunglasses on.

Sure enough there was a Santa sitting in a dusty green truck with a handicap tag, staring at people as they moved in and around him.

"Yeah, he's not very subtle. Most people are on their phones. Maybe that's why he stands out so much."

Aileen didn't glance in his direction as they walked directly by his truck, scooting to the side to let a teenage couple past them.

"Ooh, he's following," Elli said. "Dante and Theo are behind us, said he got out right after us." Her voice was so low Aileen could barely hear it above the pounding in her ears.

She knew this had been her idea, but she was still nervous because anything could happen. But no, she had this.

"I'll get in the driver's side, then you pop the trunk, leave the cart and head to the front seat as if you're putting the bag in."

"Got it." Heart still pounding as they made their way through the packed parking lot, she left her fake purse in the cart and did exactly what Elli had said. And as Aileen headed up to the front door to put her smallest bag in, the Santa made his move.

Out of the corner of her eye, she saw him dart out from the other row of cars and grab her purse and run.

"Stop, thief!" she yelled halfheartedly even as the guy darted down another row of cars. She saw him duck down out of sight, then slide into another car and peel out. It all happened so damn fast.

"Oh my god, did that guy steal your purse?" A dark-haired woman with two elementary school-aged kids asked as she popped her own trunk.

"I've already called the police." Elli said, holding up her phone.

"Oh, okay. Sorry, that sucks," the woman said as she continued loading up her bags. "People are such jerks. Don't forget to cancel all your cards, even before the cops get here."

"I will, thanks," she said even as Elli grabbed the cart and shoved it into the nearby cart holder.

As the woman drove off, Aileen slid into the passenger seat, and moments later Elli was in the driver's seat. "I don't think anyone else saw so we're going to casually get out of here."

"Are we following the guy?"

"Nope. Dante and Theo are handling that and you and I are headed home to see that sweet girl of yours."

Part of Aileen wanted to chase the jerk down, but that wasn't realistic. The pros could handle following her mugger. And hopefully this time they'd figure out what the hell was going on and who was after her.

CHAPTER 19

Time to get into the holiday spirit... Gin, vodka, whiskey.

"You expecting a call?" Theo's tone was neutral as he and Dante tailed the Santa thief through busy streets.

Dante had glanced at his phone about a hundred times so the question was fair. "Nope." Lorna had placed a tracker in the decoy purse so it was easy to tail the guy without getting too close. They were trying not to let him get too far away in case he ditched the purse. If he did, they'd still have eyes on him at least.

Theo simply grunted, then Hudson came over the comm line. "I'll take over at Laguna Street."

"Copy," Theo said. "We'll pick back up in a couple miles."

When following someone it was always better to have multiple tails so the same vehicle wasn't doing all the following. Sometimes that was unavoidable, but a lot of their neighborhood had stepped up today to help out. Everyone loved Aileen so of course they had.

Dante refused the urge to glance down at his cell. Barely... okay, lies. He looked again, wondering if maybe he'd forgotten to turn the volume back up.

"She's not going to call. She's too stubborn," Theo said as he took a left, veering away from the direction of the mugger and Hudson.

"She's not too stubborn. She's perfect." And she'd been ignoring him since yesterday morning.

Theo snort-laughed in a similar manner to the way Aileen did and Dante sighed at himself.

"You were also a little heavy-handed," Theo added.

"Says the man who kidnapped his now-wife because she was in danger."

"True." Theo gave a casual shrug. "But Elli's different. Tougher—physically. My parents, and myself to an extent, have kept Aileen in a bubble for a long time. She needed a bubble, but she's been bucking up against it and...we need to let her live her life."

"I don't want to stop her from doing anything—except running into danger."

"She wasn't running into danger though. She wasn't trying to go off and be a hero all by herself. She had a good plan, one that involved all of us backing her up, and you shot it down before even really thinking about it. Aileen knows her limits and has a good head on her shoulders. You should have respected her idea. And at least listened to it."

"You're annoying."

"I'm right."

"You're annoying when you're right."

Theo simply grinned. "True enough."

"You think she'll forgive me before Christmas?" Which was only a few days away.

"Have you actually apologized?"

Dante paused...then opened his phone up again. He scrolled through his texts, which were just requests for her to call him. In his head he'd apologized, but... "I really am a dumbass."

Theo snorted again. "I'll be sure to tell Elli you said that. And no, you're not, you're just in love."

Same difference.

A few moments later, Theo glanced at him as they pulled up to a stoplight. His expression was...difficult to read.

"What?" Dante growled.

But Theo simply shook his head slightly and turned back to look out the windshield.

Dante's finger hovered over his phone for a long moment as he debated typing out an apology. This was something he needed to do in person though. Not over the phone like some teenager. Still...

"I feel like I should give you some big brother talk about how if you hurt my sister, I'll throw you into a pit of gators. But I'm glad you guys are finally doing this thing," Theo said into the quiet. "She's lucky to have you and I'll be happy to officially call you my brother."

Theo's words made Dante freeze, his thumb over his phone. "Oh... I... We're..." He cleared his throat. He wanted everything with Aileen. A real future that involved more kids if she wanted them. Things he'd never even dared to dream of. He wanted to be a dad to Nessa, not just her favorite uncle, but the man she called when she needed help. But... "I don't know where Aileen stands...but thanks."

Theo had started to respond when Hudson came over the line. "Looks like he's starting to slow down for a stop. You guys want to take over?"

"Yep," Theo said without pause. "I see you both on the map. Moving in on Lakeview Drive."

***

Dante knew that waiting was part of any hitman's job. Or anyone in any sort of intelligence gathering. But it would never not be boring.

"You've gotta get off the phone," Dante finally growled. Because he was close to tossing Theo's cell out the window.

His friend looked at him in surprise, then said into the phone, "I'll call you later, love you."

Dante could only assume Elli said the words back before Theo hung up.

"What's up? Did you see something?" Theo followed Dante's gaze across the street where the man who'd been dressed as Santa, but was now wearing regular street clothes, sat on a bus bench.

The man—who they now knew was Vance Hull thanks to Elli's hacking skills—had taken them on a merry chase around the city all day. Though Dante didn't think it was to avoid being followed. Nope, the man had gone grocery shopping, dropped some bags off with an older woman they'd later discovered was his aunt. Then he'd met up with some friends to play pool, had strolled out of the bar and grill definitely buzzed, and proceeded to make a few more stops that all involved alcohol. Finally, he'd parked his vehicle at a shopping center a few blocks away and was now waiting at a bus stop, clearly looking for someone. Or waiting. This guy was just some loser who'd been brought in on suspicion of B&E's a handful of times. Another throwaway someone had hired.

"No, just got tired of hearing you two have phone sex."

Theo popped a jelly bean in his mouth and let his head fall back. "That's not even close to what we were doing."

"It was headed that way." He cleared his throat. "So how did you get Elliana to forgive you after kidnapping her?"

"Why? You planning on kidnapping my sister?"

"What? No." *Probably not.*

Theo shrugged and ate another disgusting jelly bean. "Sex was involved, which is something I'm sure you don't want to hear about. So you ready for the big song debut? My mom's got the karaoke machine ready to go for Christmas Eve."

"I hate you both," he muttered, but straightened when an older model blue Cadillac slowed in front of the bus stop.

Dante pulled out his long-range camera, started snapping pictures as Vance stood, glanced around, then reached into his backpack. He pulled out the stolen purse, then leaned down to talk to whoever was in the car. When he stood a few moments later it was sans purse, but he was holding an envelope. He shoved his hands and envelope in his jacket pockets and headed south as the vehicle drove north.

Theo waited a moment and they both watched as the dot headed off in the same direction of the car. As soon as the driver made a right turn, Theo started up and headed out.

"I'm sending the license plate to Elliana," Dante murmured. They already had the name of the mugger and knew his address. That guy wasn't going anywhere. He was simply a thief who'd been doing a job. And if Dante had to guess, he was headed to the nearest bar to keep the party going the rest of the night.

This Caddy driver was the one who'd hired him.

They followed the driver until the Cadillac pulled into a Publix parking lot. By the time they caught up, Dante figured the person must be shopping. But... "Do you see the vehicle anywhere?" It was a packed parking lot, but not so big that a giant blue Caddy wouldn't stick out.

"No." Theo's voice was tight as he cruised down another aisle of parked vehicles. "Shit, look." He chin nodded to one of the built-in garbage receptacles at the end of the aisle.

The purse lay tossed on top, whoever had done it not even bothering to shove it inside fully.

"You see anyone watching?" Dante asked, glancing around.

"No, but just risk it anyway," Theo murmured as he slowed in front of it.

Dante moved fast, snagging the purse before sliding back into the vehicle in moments. But there was nothing inside. The burner phone they'd used as a decoy was gone and so was the faux wallet.

"Elli's calling," Theo said, putting his phone on speaker.

"I found the owner of the car." Her voice came through the vehicle's Bluetooth loud and clear. "That rude bitch from the store today, Linda True."

CHAPTER 20

If a fat man puts you in a bag at night, don't worry. I told Santa I want you for Christmas.

Sitting at Theo and Elliana's kitchen countertop, Dante looked over the spread of information on Linda True. She was a mom of three kids ages eleven, twelve and thirteen. Stairsteps.

She'd gone into business with a friend a few years ago selling refurbished or thrifted items worth way more than they'd found them for, and they'd turned their idea into a multimillion-dollar business. Her husband had quit his job and did small contract work at home, mostly IT stuff. But he was the one who hauled the kids around everywhere, took them to their doctors' appointments and such. He drove a hybrid SUV and she drove a little car.

The Cadillac had belonged to her dad, and according to the records Elliana had found, she kept it in a storage locker off Brickell. So she'd been careful not to use something that obviously belonged to them, but likely hadn't counted on anyone following the guy she'd hired.

"She must think Aileen is having an affair with her husband, but why would she want her phone? She'd want her husband's phone," Dante murmured as he pulled up another tab. This one was simply of the woman's phone records so he turned away from the laptop.

"Maybe...ugh, I don't know." And Elliana looked pissed about it.

Since it was late and Aileen was having a movie night with Nessa, they'd opted not to include her in this. No sense in ruining her night with her daughter when Dante, Elliana and Theo could handle looking over information.

And at least they finally had a name to go with this nonsense.

"Have you found any connections between the True woman and the gang member who reached out to Adam Jackson?" The first Santa.

"Not yet, but she—or her company—has done a lot of business so there could be any number of connections there. And her business partner is from the same neighborhood-ish as the guy who hired Jackson. Not saying that's a connection, but it's not nothing. I'm going to work on this angle tonight."

"I can help," Dante said. Aileen and Nessa would be asleep now and he didn't want to go home just yet. She hadn't asked him to stay over, but had promised to set her alarm. Her promise to do that had made it clear that he wasn't invited over to her place.

Which cut deep, but he'd brought it on himself. She needed space and he could appreciate that. Sort of.

Okay, not at all.

He wanted to be in her bed holding her, keeping her safe and happy and...ugh. It was going to be a long, stupid night.

Pulling out his phone, he texted Sarah, who was sitting on the Trues' house. Linda True must have ditched the phone somewhere too because it had gone offline not long after she'd tossed the purse. She'd gotten what she wanted so hopefully this was the end of whatever was going on.

But they weren't taking any chances. *Any changes?* he texted.

Nope.

That was about as much as he was going to get from Sarah so he set his phone down and sighed. Tomorrow morning, he was going over to Aileen's place and apologizing in person. Then he was going to give her so many orgasms that she would just have to forgive him.

CHaPTeR 21

It's all fun and games until Santa checks the naughty list.

Aileen opened her fridge even though it was two in the morning and she wasn't hungry at all. But she couldn't sleep.

Not talking to Dante, not clearing the air, was eating her up inside. But it was more than that. There was something nagging her that she couldn't put her finger on. She'd remember eventually, but until she did it was going to drive her crazy.

She knew from Theo that he and Dante had watched the Santa exchange the stolen purse for what looked like an envelope of cash. And that Linda True was the owner of the Cadillac.

And Aileen couldn't figure out why this woman had taken issue with her or why she wanted her phone. She barely knew Calvin True, had only talked to him at soccer games or practices. And usually she used that time to walk or jog around the neighboring fields. It wasn't like she interacted much with any of the parents. Come to think of it, neither did Calvin.

At that, she paused as she shut the refrigerator.

She'd seen Calvin True leaving practices before instead of waiting for his daughter. A lot of parents did, usually to run errands or to cook dinner at home or whatever. But some stayed, and he was hit or miss.

As she thought about it...maybe that was what was bothering her. Had she seen him driving an Eldorado Cadillac? Theo had sent her a picture of it a few hours ago and ever since then something had been bothering her.

They'd never seen Linda True driving it so they were simply assuming it had been her based on her being the owner. She needed to check her phone—which was upstairs.

She'd taken tons of pictures over the last few months at practices and games. If he'd ever driven the thing, it would be in one of them.

As she headed back toward the hallway, all the lights went out and silence filled the air. She froze at the sound of a little thump. The steady hmm of her refrigerator and freezer were no longer background noise. There was nothing now.

On quiet feet, she headed toward the living room instead of upstairs. Using the light from outside as her guide, she moved to the big window and eased the curtains back.

Her entire neighborhood had gone dark. All the front yard decorations had dimmed. One neighbor had a few lights flickering... The generator. They all had them, but hers was hooked up in the garage. This was probably just an outage but...there wasn't any bad weather and she hadn't heard a transformer blow.

Heart pounding, she turned and hurried through her dark house. She needed to get to her phone and to check on Nessa.

Something didn't feel right.

As she reached the bottom of her stairs, she turned at a slight noise and found herself looking down the barrel of a pistol and a flashlight.

CHAPTER 22

Dear Santa, I've been good-ish this year.

Something was wrong. Dante felt it in his bones the moment the neighborhood went dark.

Going on instinct, he slipped out his front door and hurried down the sidewalk to Aileen's house. Unable to sleep, he'd been watching her house like a stalker because apparently he *was* one. Didn't matter that they had the True residence under surveillance.

He needed eyes on Aileen, to know she was safe.

As he made his way toward her house, he texted her. No response. Which...could be nothing. It was two in the morning. As he reached the side of her house he debated calling, but then stopped himself. He would just check things out, make sure his girls were okay. That was it.

As he reached the side of the garage, he stilled.

Footprints that hadn't been there earlier in the evening tracked around the house leading right up to the side door that led to the garage. She rarely used it—hell, he was pretty sure she had a couple bins of decorations stacked against it.

He shot off a group text to Lorna, Theo and Nestor before he approached the side door, pistol in hand. The lock had been picked. And the camera above the door wasn't lighting up from the motion of him stepping under it.

Easing to the side, he slowly opened the door then swept into the garage, flashlight in one hand, pistol in the other.

The bins had been shoved to the side, but the garage was empty.

Moving quickly, he hurried to the door to the mudroom, saw similar scratch marks on the door. He eased it open, found the small room empty.

Turning off his flashlight now, he used his knowledge of her house to his advantage as he quietly opened the door that connected to the kitchen.

Muted voices trailed to him. Aileen and someone else.

He focused on the sound of their voices as he forced himself to remain calm. To fall back on all his training.

Aileen's life depended on it.

"You haven't done anything wrong, Calvin." Aileen's voice shook but she sounded calm. "Just put your gun down and leave and I'll never tell anyone."

"Everything's gone to shit. I got rid of all the video evidence, but then saw you with your stupid phone, recording your daughter! I can't... I can't do this anymore. I need it all to be over. I need your phone!" he snarled.

Dante moved quickly through the kitchen toward the voices. They had to be in the living room or foyer, so very close. All he needed was a clean shot and this guy was dead.

"Someone stole my phone earlier today. I don't have it."

"Bullshit, bullshit," he repeated, his voice unsteady. "I have your purse but it wasn't your phone. You have a sparkly case and that was some basic burner bullshit. I *need* your phone."

Dante moved around the island, the voices growing louder. Her kitchen connected to the hallway and foyer, which led to the stairs. There was another way around it through a dining room, but he needed the element of surprise. This asshole had a weapon so Dante had to be careful. One wrong shot... No, he wouldn't let his mind go there. He was a pro and now all his training would come in handy for the most important moment of his life.

"Okay, fine, it's in the kitchen, we just need to get it. Why do you need my phone so badly?"

"You know why."

"I really don't."

"Oh god, it's all falling apart." Calvin's voice trembled even worse. "Walk that way, now. In front of me and don't try anything stupid."

Dante flattened himself up against the wall next to the pantry door, thankful for the darkness. It was the only thing that would help him blend in.

"Keep your hands up," the walking dead man snarled a moment before Aileen walked into her kitchen right past Dante, her hands up and out.

"I left it on the countertop over there," she said, motioning to where he knew a bowl that had pepper spray sat. They were in the bowl underneath a bunch of things she tossed at the end of the day.

The man moved into Dante's line of sight, his weapon hand out, a flashlight tucked under it, pointing straight at Aileen's back.

Hell. No.

Dante moved in behind him, grabbed his weapon arm and lifted it fast, breaking Calvin's bone in a vicious snap.

The man was fit, struggled for a moment as he let out a short scream of pain, but Dante had years of training as a killer. He broke his neck in a few quick moves, the pistol falling with a clatter next to him.

"Oh my god," Aileen breathed out even as Dante eased the man to the floor.

"Where's Nessa?"

"She should be okay but I need to check on her." Her eyes were wide as she stared at the dead body for a long moment, then she snapped out of it and hurried for the stairs.

Dante went with her, leading the way with his pistol in case there was anyone else in her house. But the house was empty other than them.

Nessa was sleeping on her side, with the kind of steady breathing of a kid who knows they're safe. As it should be.

"We need to get rid of the body," Dante said once they were back in the hallway. "Before she wakes up."

Aileen nodded, moving fast with him as they hurried down the stairs.

"Did he hurt you?" he asked as they reached the bottom.

She was already shaking her head as they made it to the kitchen—where her family was waiting.

"I'll get a tarp," Theo said before Dante could ask.

"And I've already called the cleanup crew," Lorna added.

"Nessa?" Nestor asked.

"Sleeping."

Nestor nodded, looked between the two of them, then nodded again. His girls were safe, something Dante understood. They'd figure out what the hell was going on later, but for now... He wrapped his arms around Aileen and pulled her out into the hallway, thankful when she moved with him without question.

She buried her face against his chest, breathed deep. "I thought..."

"I'll always be there for you," he growled. "Nothing happened and nothing would have happened. You'd have handled shit with that pepper spray."

She let out a strangled-sounding laugh as she nodded into his chest. Then she pulled back slightly, her voice pitched low in the dim hallway. "I'd planned to spray him but I'm glad...I'm glad you were here."

"I should have been here all night. I'm sorry for the way I acted before. For the record you're one of the smartest people I know, and I know you thought everything through. I was just worried and didn't want you rushing into danger and I acted like a giant asshole."

"You don't need to do this now," she murmured, still holding him close.

"Yeah, I do. I was wrong. It's not an excuse, but I was worried about your safety and my brain went to the worst-case scenario. I got scared."

"Scared?"

"The thought of losing you terrifies the hell out of me. It's the worst possible scenario in every situation. And I love you, Aileen." Belatedly he realized that he probably shouldn't be telling her not far from a dead body.

Of a guy he'd just killed.

In front of her. But, too late now.

"Don't feel like—" He started.

"Please don't finish that," she whispered, going up on tiptoe to kiss him. "I love you too. I've loved you for...a lot longer than I wanted to admit to myself. For so long I was scared to open myself up, to be vulnerable to anyone but my family. And then you came along. And I was lost, even if it took me a while to get here."

He threaded his hands through the back of her hair as he gently leaned down to kiss her, to claim her mouth...but pulled back when he heard the cleaning crew arrive.

There would be time enough for this later and he didn't want to start something he couldn't finish anyway.

Because he was going to take his time with Aileen. There was still one thing he needed to tell her before they moved on to the next level in their relationship. But for now, he would focus on what he could actually help with.

CHAPTER 23

Dear Santa, is it too late to start trying?

Aileen slid onto the stool at her island top, glad the "cleaners" were gone and that body was out of her house. She didn't even want to think about what could have happened if Nessa had woken up... Nausea threatened but she swallowed it back. No sense in traveling down that path.

Dante kissed her forehead as he slid coffee in front of her—and no one in her family batted an eye at their little display of affection.

Of course, her family rarely acted surprised at anything, and only an hour ago there had been a dead man in her kitchen. She was just glad that Dante hadn't shot him so there was no blood to clean up.

And oh my god, she hated herself for thinking that but whatever. She wanted to keep her daughter protected.

"Until we've decided things, the cleaners are going to keep the body preserved," her mom said, leaning against the nearby countertop.

"Good," Aileen murmured as she pulled out her cell phone. "And I know why he was here. I realized it when he drew the pistol on me."

Dante made a dark, growling sound.

She ignored him as she pulled her cell phone out and started scrolling through pictures. "Something had been bothering me but I couldn't figure out what it was. But there was just something nagging me..." She found what she was looking for and set her phone on the countertop. "Look at the background in this one, then look at the video background of the next. Just swipe left."

Everyone crowded together and she watched as one by one their eyes widened.

Calvin True was in the background of a couple photos and one video with Christina Fraser, the murdered teacher who'd been all over the news for the last month.

"The video is from the day she disappeared. It was earlier in the day, but according to her friends and at least one coworker, they were pretty sure she was having an affair with a married man."

"Oh. My. God." Elliana had her laptop out even as she spoke.

Aileen watched again as this time Dante pulled it up. Nessa was popping her soccer ball up on her knees, and sure enough, in the background of the parking lot was Christina Fraser sitting in the passenger seat of Calvin True's vehicle. Or his wife's Cadillac, to be more specific. That was what had been bothering her.

The car.

When Theo had mentioned the car they'd been following, it had struck something in her memory, but she couldn't remember what. Now she did. She hadn't been close enough to see the Fraser woman, and it wasn't clear who she was until Aileen zoomed in. Then the woman's face and hair were clear. "How did he even know I took this?" From the angle, he wasn't paying attention to anything other than the woman in his passenger seat. They made out briefly before he pulled away from the parking spot and tore out of there.

"I heard him say something earlier," Dante murmured as he set her phone back down. "He said, 'I got rid of all the video evidence, but then saw you with your stupid phone, recording your daughter.' Or something to that effect. If he got rid of video evidence, he could have been talking about the security feeds at the community center, the soccer fields. That's where you took this video. And if he destroyed the videos, he would have seen you recording. And the angle makes it obvious it was trained in his direction. It seems clear that he was having an affair with the Fraser woman, and whether he murdered her or not, he didn't want to risk their relationship getting out."

"He broke into my house and wanted to kill me for my phone. Pretty sure he killed the woman." Which was why Aileen felt a lot less guilty about the whole thing.

"Agreed." And Dante didn't look like he felt one ounce of guilt.

"I'll find out soon enough," Elli said from across the island top. "Not this morning, but I'm going to make some calls. The police will definitely want to know about their relationship and..." Elli shook her head. "This is going to tear apart his family."

Aileen nodded, a heavy weight settling in her gut. "He had three kids. Girls. No wonder his wife thought we were affair partners or whatever. She must have known he was having an affair and thought it was me." Maybe because she'd run into him at the gala and he'd looked surprised. Or maybe horrified. Then Aileen had run into him at that Christmas store— Nope, she hadn't run into him. He'd clearly been watching her videos. He'd made it seem like they ran into each other. "Oh my god," she muttered. "He must have planted something on me yesterday. A tracker or something." It was the only explanation for how he'd found her, because her home wasn't in her name.

"Where are the clothes you were wearing?" her mom asked.

"My jacket is hanging up in the laundry room."

Her mom disappeared, then was back moments later, already feeling around for something on her black pullover. Moments later she paused, then ran her fingers over the pocket a couple times before pulling out a flat little disc smaller than a dime. Her mom's lips pulled into a thin line. "This is pretty high-tech stuff."

"Yeah, we've seen it surging," Elli said, nodding along. "Well, it explains how he found you and why the power in the neighborhood went off."

They knew that someone had taken out two transformers, which had sent everyone in the neighborhood into lockdown essentially. Calvin True wouldn't have known he'd targeted a neighborhood full of hitmen, wouldn't have realized the chaos he'd set off inside all the quiet houses.

"So what are we going to do?" Aileen asked into the quiet lull.

"I'll see what I can find as far as video evidence from the community fields. If he really did somehow manage to get rid of it, then we'll go from there. But we've got video proof of their relationship on your phone. We can anonymously give it to the cops... And make it so the cops find his body?" Elli asked, looking at Theo.

Theo nodded. "Yeah, we can maybe make his broken neck look like an accident. If we send him and his car over a bridge, it could be believable. After that, it's not up to us to do the job for the police. They'll have the evidence of his relationship and I'm sure from there they'll be able to unravel more."

Aileen nodded even as she stifled a yawn. Nessa would be up in a couple hours and Aileen wanted to grab some sleep before then.

"All right, everyone out. Aileen needs to rest," Dante said suddenly. Authoritatively. "We'll meet up later and discuss everything, but unless you need her or me, we're getting some sleep."

Ooooh, she loved that he just took over, that he'd basically read her mind about wanting to crash. Or at least he'd been paying attention to her yawning. Either way, she really did love the man.

CHAPTER 24

Dear Santa, sorry I ate all your cookies.

Christmas Eve

Aileen grinned as Dante finished his rendition of Springsteen's "Dancing in the Dark" before taking a bow in front of her fireplace. Since they'd already had the big neighborhood party with everyone, families tended to do their own thing on Christmas Eve.

Tonight it was Aileen, Nessa, Dante, Theo and Elli, and of course Nestor and Lorna.

Theo and Elli would be heading out soon for another party—one Nessa was jealous she couldn't go to. But Elli had promised that next year she could go to the Christmas Eve party at superstar Rebel Martinez's house.

Rebel had actually invited Elli's "new family" but Aileen couldn't handle a crowd tonight. Not even to visit Rebel's place. She was still reeling from everything, and even though they now had more details, it was a lot to process.

That a man who'd she'd been relatively friendly with had tried to kill her because of his crimes.

"You were amazing," she said as Dante strode toward her in his Rudolph-themed Christmas sweater.

He actually flushed as he grinned. "Were you recording me?"

"You better believe it because you looked good up there." And the man truly was a great singer. Of course he was. She swore that he was talented at everything.

He groaned, but didn't say anything. He made a move to pull her into his arms but stopped when Nessa raced up, her glow in the dark helmet in place. They still hadn't told her about the two of them, were waiting until after Christmas to see how she felt about the change.

"I want to go ride my bike since I have to miss the party of the year. Of the *century*!" she added with the dramatic flair of an eleven-year-old.

"I'll go with her." Dante paused, looking a whole lot like he wanted to kiss Aileen, but headed off with Nessa talking about her cool new helmet—and how when she was a grown-up no one was going to tell her what to do.

They'd all exchanged one gift tonight, played games, sang karaoke, ate too much food, and now everything was winding down.

"I heard back from my contact," Elli said as she picked up her bag of gifts. "Calvin True paid off someone to remove a couple hours of video at the community fields. Told him it was because he was having an affair and didn't want his wife to know. He worked with the guy five years ago before his wife's business took off. Guy said he removed them, but didn't fully delete them 'just in case.' I think he planned to blackmail him or something later, but either way, the evidence of Calvin with Christina Fraser is there. And now that the cops have it, they're unraveling even more."

Aileen shook her head slightly, not surprised. It was hard to keep a secret like that.

Elli continued as Theo took her bag from her, hoisted it onto his shoulder. "They've also discovered that Calvin was taking his wife's Caddy from storage so he could sneak around with Fraser. I guess it was close to a couple places he dropped the kids off during the week and that way there wasn't a record of where he'd been going. His current vehicle has a tracking system that apparently his wife was using to keep tabs on him. Because it's not the first time he had an affair. She told him if he cheated again, she was done, and he believed her."

"How do you know all that?"

"She told the cops when they questioned her. She's distraught, of course, and even mentioned yelling at a 'random woman' the other day because she thought you were having an affair with her husband. It'll be hard for her family for a while, but she'll be better off without him."

"And at least Christina Fraser's parents have closure."

"Yeah." Elli nodded, looking pensive for a moment, but then her expression cleared. "I'm just glad you're okay. Thank you for the party tonight. I wish this was where my night was ending."

Aileen snorted softly. "Liar. You're going to have so much fun at Rebel's."

"She's not lying," Theo murmured, kissing the top of Aileen's head. "She'll complain the whole way, then cuddle with their dogs the entire time we're there."

Elli just grinned and shrugged, not denying it.

After they left, Aileen hugged her parents, only to be stopped by her dad in the foyer.

"Are you good?" he murmured, watching her closely.

"Yeess," she drew the word out, wondering where this was going. "Why?"

"I know a lot has happened and I just wanted to check. You're still my little girl."

"I'm good, I promise." Or as good as she was going to be. She was still a little unsettled, but she had her family, and Dante. Dante, the man she loved more than she ever could have imagined. "Are you okay with me and Dante? Not that I'm asking for permission or anything," she added, wanting that very clear.

He just grinned. "I'm happy you two finally figured things out. He's a perfect fit for you."

She blinked in surprise, but then he kissed her forehead and headed out the front door.

She followed after him to find Nessa riding around the end of the cul-de-sac in circles with one of her best friends, singing "Jingle Bells" at the top of their lungs.

Laughing, Aileen sidled up to Dante, determined to tell Nessa tomorrow or maybe the day after Christmas. "Is it weird that this is the best Christmas Eve I remember having?"

"Nope." He grinned down at her, the love in his eyes so clear she couldn't believe it had taken her so long to see it.

He was definitely it for her too.

CHAPTER 25

I'm only a morning person on December 25th.

Christmas Day

Nessa carefully stepped into the living room and froze when she saw her mom and Dante sleeping on the couch, Dante with his arms around her mom.

There were a bunch of new presents under the tree, including a sparkly purple bike she'd had her eye on. But the best present of all—Dante had spent the night.

And he was holding on to her mom really close. Just like a dad would.

She knew it! Santa hadn't let her down.

As she stood there, they both opened their eyes almost at the same time, her mom blinking sleepily. "Hey hon, Merry Christmas. We, uh...we just fell asleep, I guess..."

Dante cleared his throat, his dark hair all messy. "Yeah, we must have—"

"It's okay. You don't have to make anything up. I know the truth."

Now they both blinked. "You do?" her mom asked, looking almost a little panicked.

But she wasn't sure why. "Uh, yeah. I asked Santa—and Elli—for a new dad." She looked at Dante expectantly. "It's okay if you sleep over here. If you're going to be my dad, you'll have to move in anyway."

Her mom stared at her now, her mouth slightly open.

But Dante simply nodded in agreement. Good, he wasn't trying to keep anything from her. God, adults were so weird. She knew things would work out between them. It only made sense. Dante loved her mom and her mom definitely loved Dante.

"Wait, you told Elli you wanted a new dad?" Her mom sat up a little straighter, as if she was going to stand, but Dante pulled her back into his lap.

Oh, they were totally together.

"Yep, and we came up with a plan to get you guys together. It's why I was talking about that guy you went on a date with. Elli said that it would make Dante jealous. And it did."

Dante's mouth fell open a little now. "Wait, you were involved in Elliana's shenanigans?"

"You knew what Elli was up to?" Aileen elbowed Dante, who simply shrugged.

"Can I open presents now? And maybe now is a good time to ask for some siblings. They could be here by next Christmas," she said as she dove in front of the tree and picked up a sparkling gold package with her name on it. At this point everything else was just a bonus present.

She'd gotten a new dad for Christmas.

One she knew her mom was never letting go. She just hoped they gave her some siblings later. She really wanted a little sister. Or, like, three. She and her mom had done so many fun things over the last decade, but it was time to make the family bigger. Elli had joined theirs and that had turned out amazing. More girls would be even better.

And Nessa needed someone to teach things to anyway. Because girls were gonna rule the world one day.

***

Dante helped set out the plates on Aileen's counter in preparation for the group coming over soon.

"So...this morning went better than expected." Aileen kept her voice pitched low as she pulled the breakfast casserole out of the oven. Nessa wasn't back from her grandparents' yet, but Aileen didn't seem to be taking any chances.

Dante took over immediately, setting the casserole out of the way before he pulled her into his arms. God, he couldn't get enough of touching her. Everyone would be over soon for breakfast but he was savoring the quiet moment while it was just the two of them.

After helping her wrap presents last night, they'd fallen asleep while watching a Christmas movie. And he never wanted to sleep anywhere else but holding her. On the couch, the floor, in bed—didn't matter. As long as she was happy and comfortable.

"Apparently Elliana doesn't hate me after all," he murmured, brushing his mouth over Aileen's.

She grinned against him. "Apparently not. But we're going to have to watch out for those two. They're both sneaky and Elli will only encourage Nessa's mischievous streak."

Happier than he ever remembered being, he found himself laughing at the utter truth of that. "So...how do you feel about giving Nessa siblings?"

Aileen's green eyes went wide, then she blinked a couple times. "Um...maybe we wait a year? I'd like some time with just the three of us."

"Anytime you're ready," he growled even as he reached into his pants pocket and pulled out the box he'd been holding onto for way too long. He might be able to wait for kids, but he couldn't wait to put his claim on Aileen.

"Seriously?" She hadn't pulled back. If anything, she was pressed up against him even closer.

He leaned against the countertop with her plastered against him and his gaze automatically strayed to her mouth. They didn't have time to do anything before the others showed up, but that didn't stop him from fantasizing. "I want kids with you. I want to wake up to your gorgeous face every morning. I want to be a dad to Nessa, officially. I want..." He lifted her left hand and slid the sparkly engagement ring on her ring finger. "...everything."

She stared down at the ring, then back up at him in a bit of shock. Then she grinned and it was a punch to his solar plexus. "So you're not even asking, huh?"

No point. "If you said no, I'd probably take a page out of Theo's book and kidnap you."

"You're not even lying right now," she murmured, leaning up to kiss him again. "How would you convince me to marry you?" she whispered.

He reached between her legs, covered her unfortunately jean-clad mound with his big hand. "I'd spend a lot of time down here..." He nipped her bottom lip. "...making you come so hard that you'd have to say yes."

She groaned slightly. "As soon as everyone leaves today, we're getting naked."

Maybe even sooner... "I need to tell you something," he finally forced out. Because he wanted to start this relationship—soon to be marriage—with full honesty.

She quirked an eyebrow. "That sounds a little ominous."

"I...used to watch your ASMR videos. Before...I knew you. I mean, I *still* watch them." That wasn't so much a confession as the first part.

She blinked. "What?"

"I watched your videos when you were first starting out. I stumbled across them one night when I couldn't sleep. I didn't know you were Lorna and Nestor's daughter. I found that out later... It's why I moved to the neighborhood."

She blinked again and he couldn't read her.

"Not in a weird way or...maybe it was. But your videos helped me sleep when nothing else did." He'd been in a dark place when he'd discovered her videos. "You saved me and helped pull me out of a bad head space." He'd loved listening to her rambling, talking about everything and nothing. She'd been so sweet and charming—still was.

"I don't even know what to say," she whispered.

But she wasn't pulling away so that was something.

"When I found out that you were their daughter..." He lifted a shoulder. "I moved here to be closer to you. I figured if you helped me, you were helping a lot of other people too. And I wanted to be close to you...to keep you safe." And okay, he'd already been a little bit obsessed with her.

She leaned up on tiptoe and kissed him hard before pulling back. "I love you, Dante. And for the record, I *will* marry you."

Relief punched through him that she wasn't horrified by his secret, one he'd been carrying for too long. "Maybe I'll kidnap you anyway," he murmured before he claimed her mouth again.

But soon the front door banged open and voices filled the air as everyone came stomping in, talking and laughing.

"See! I told you I got a new dad for Christmas. Pay up, Uncle Theo!" Nessa was holding out her palm as Theo slapped a twenty in it, grinning even as he parted with his money.

Lorna saw the ring first, her eagle-eyed gaze narrowing in on it before she looked at Dante and nodded once in approval.

And hell yeah, he would take it. At the end of the day, he didn't care what anyone but Aileen or Nessa thought, but he was glad Aileen's family approved.

Because they'd become his family over the years and soon he'd make it official. He fake stumbled back when Nessa raced at him, hugging him hard around the waist.

"This is the best Christmas ever!" she shouted up at him, clearly only having one volume today. Loud.

And he loved it. "Agreed, nugget."

"It really is." Aileen slid her arm around his middle, and when she looked up at him, he felt more at peace than he ever had. "Merry Christmas."

She was the missing piece he hadn't even known he needed. But she and Nessa had filled a void inside him. And even if he didn't deserve them, he would spend the rest of his life taking care of them, cherishing them the way they deserved. "Merry Christmas, baby."

Dear Readers

I hope you enjoyed this latest holiday romp! The next in the series will involve a mischievous llama so stay tuned. If you'd like to stay in touch and be the first to learn about new releases you can:

Check out my website for book news: https://www.katiereus.com

Also, please consider leaving a review at one of your favorite online retailers. It's a great way to help other readers discover new books and I appreciate all reviews.

Happy reading,
Katie

ACKnOWLeDGemenTs

My pups Piper and Jack are getting a shout out for this one! They're with me every day as I work and are the best company a writer could ask for. Thank you for forcing me out in the sunshine when I'd rather live like a vampire. I'm also grateful to Julia for editing another holiday story, to Jaycee for another wonderful cover and to Tammy for line edits. The three of you are wonderful! For Sarah, thank you for all the things, ever, until the end of time. I'm also incredibly thankful for my mom, who gave me my love of Christmas (without the hitmen). And for you, my wonderful readers, who asked for more in this world. Thank you for reading my books. I'm so grateful to all of you.

ABOUT THe AUTHOr

Katie Reus is the *USA Today* bestselling author of the Red Stone Security series, the Ancients Rising series and the Redemption Harbor series. She fell in love with romance at a young age thanks to books she pilfered from her mom's stash. Years later she loves reading romance almost as much as she loves writing it.

However, she didn't always know she wanted to be a writer. After changing majors many times, she finally graduated summa cum laude with a degree in psychology. Not long after that she discovered a new love. Writing. She now spends her days writing paranormal romance and sexy romantic suspense.

COMPLETE BOOKLIST

Sentinel of Darkness
A Very Dragon Christmas
Darkness Rising

Deadly Ops Series
Targeted
Bound to Danger
Chasing Danger
Shattered Duty
Edge of Danger
A Covert Affair

Endgame Trilogy
Bishop's Knight
Bishop's Queen
Bishop's Endgame

Holiday With a Hitman Series
How the Hitman Stole Christmas
A Very Merry Hitman
All I Want for Christmas is a Hitman

MacArthur Family Series
Falling for Irish
Unintended Target
Saving Sienna

Moon Shifter Series
Alpha Instinct
Lover's Instinct
Primal Possession

Mating Instinct

His Untamed Desire

Avenger's Heat

Hunter Reborn

Protective Instinct

Dark Protector

A Mate for Christmas

O'Connor Family Series

Merry Christmas, Baby

Tease Me, Baby

It's Me Again, Baby

Mistletoe Me, Baby

Red Stone Security Series®

No One to Trust

Danger Next Door

Fatal Deception

Miami, Mistletoe & Murder

His to Protect

Breaking Her Rules

Protecting His Witness

Sinful Seduction

Under His Protection

Deadly Fallout

Sworn to Protect

Secret Obsession

Love Thy Enemy

Dangerous Protector

Lethal Game

Secret Enemy

Saving Danger

Guarding Her

Deadly Protector

Danger Rising

Protecting Rebel

Redemption Harbor® Series

Resurrection

Savage Rising

Dangerous Witness

Innocent Target

Hunting Danger

Covert Games

Chasing Vengeance

Redemption Harbor® Security

Fighting for Hailey

Fighting for Reese

Fighting for Adalyn

Fighting for Magnolia

Fighting for Berlin

Sin City Series (the Serafina)

First Surrender

Sensual Surrender

Sweetest Surrender

Dangerous Surrender

Deadly Surrender

Verona Bay Series

Dark Memento

Deadly Past

Silent Protector

Linked books

Retribution

Tempting Danger

Non-series Romantic Suspense

Running From the Past

Dangerous Secrets

Killer Secrets

Deadly Obsession

Danger in Paradise

His Secret Past

The Trouble with Rylee

Falling for Nola

Tempted by Her Neighbor

Falling for Valentine

Paranormal Romance

Destined Mate

Protector's Mate

A Jaguar's Kiss

Tempting the Jaguar

Enemy Mine

Heart of the Jaguar

www.ingramcontent.com/pod-product-compliance
Lightning Source LLC
Chambersburg PA
CBHW050452110726
47899CB00003B/914